Baby For Daddy's Best Friend

Callie Stevens

Chapter 1

Rye

It's good to be home. I've missed Chicago. After spending the past seven years in Wisconsin, I'm ready to be back in the city I love.

The car rolls up to the brick townhouse with the black door. We moved in when I was in sixth grade. Mom and Dad were going to downsize, but after Mom passed away my second year of college, Dad hasn't had the heart to let go of it. I'm glad for it.

I get out of the car and thank the driver as he fetches my bags. There's a chill in the air. March in Chicago is still practically the depths of winter. But I don't care. Standing before the house, I can't help but smile. Although, it's bittersweet.

On one hand, I'm moving back home to get a grip on my life. The flower shop I have been working at since college finally closed down. A mom-and-pop place, the best in the region. I was apprenticing with them and cut my teeth arranging flowers for weddings and events. I'd come to love the store as my own and even asked the owners, Aggy and

Tim, if I could buy the business off of them. But no. "All good things must come to an end," Aggy had said with a crinkling smile.

Too bad it doesn't even feel like *my* good things have gotten started.

On the other, though, my dad is getting married. I know for most kids, this sounds like a nightmare. But he's been alone so long, what with me going to college and then losing Mom... Giselle is good for both of us. They met in a group for people grieving loved ones who passed away from cancer. She'd just lost her sister. It's funny how loss brings people together like that.

I don't understand what Giselle sees in my dad when she's so gorgeous: tall and lithe with a dark complexion. My dad's... well, he's my dad. Ten years her senior, with graying hair, softening around the jaw.

But man, they really love each other.

The front door flies open and Giselle appears, her broad smile sparkling. "Clay! My favorite person is here!"

Giselle has always treated me more like a best friend than a new mother. She rushes down the stairs and meets me at the gate before I can even take a step forward, throwing her arms around me. I laugh and hug her back, taking in a big inhale of the coconut oil in her braids.

"Show me the ring, show me the ring!" I squeal and grab her by the hand. Dad did a nice job. Simple, clean. A sapphire. Bright blue.

Giselle laughs at my gawking and wraps her hands around my face, brown eyes examining every bit of me. "I'm so happy you're here."

"*We're* so happy," Dad calls out from the top of the steps.

I leave Giselle's embrace and go to hug my dad, just as I did as a child. Excitedly and fully. "Hi, Daddy."

"Hi, kiddo."

We all make our way inside where lunch is waiting for me. Giselle and Dad are always cooking new recipes, obsessed with cooking shows and collecting cookbooks. "This looks amazing," I say as we sit. I eat nonstop for ten minutes. Something about eating food cooked for you by loved ones is so much better than cooking for yourself. "So, tell me everything."

Giselle folds her hands under her chin and regards my dad with loving eyes. "Well... we want to get married as soon as possible."

"But we have to have a wedding," Dad says firmly.

Giselle rolls her eyes. "I want to elope, but your father is *traditional,* apparently."

"We have to have a wedding. I'm sorry, baby."

"You're probably the only woman in the world not interested in having a wedding, Giselle."

She swipes her hand through the air. "I don't understand all the to do. It's just compulsory."

I giggle. Giselle is an anthropologist. She's always indicting frivolous cultural traditions.

"In an effort to appease Giselle, though, I've agreed to a shotgun wedding."

Giselle glowers. "Six months is *not* a 'shotgun wedding', Clay."

"Most engagements last years these days!"

"Which is ridiculous given the state of health insurance," I remark.

Giselle points at me. "Exactly."

"Ganging up on me already, I see," Dad mumbles. I know he secretly loves it, though.

"Anyway, since your father's insisting this be a big white wedding, I was wondering if maybe you would be willing to take up the wedding planning. I don't much care about all the details other than the fact he shows up."

Dad laughs. "Oh, I'll be there." He looks at me with a smile. "I just thought since you'll have a bit of free time before we start really getting your flower shop up and running... "

I roll my eyes. My dad is adamant about giving me the capital to start up my own florist here in the city. It means the world to me, really. I just can't help but feel a little embarrassed. Not everyone has the means to follow their dreams like I do. I'm very blessed.

"Plus, we're obviously going to have you design the flower arrangements. That way you can make some connections and—"

I stop eating and regard them both with big eyes. "Really?"

"Of course!" he replies. "Who else would we ask?"

"You really want me to... " I touch my heart. I shouldn't be as surprised as I am, but I'm completely taken aback.

Dad nods toward his fiancée. "It was Giselle's idea."

I look at her. I love this woman. Really. If I can't have my Mom with me... this is the next best thing. "You're the best, Elle."

She shrugs, but her lips are smug. "I thought it was only natural to ask my maid of honor to show off her talents for all to see."

Now, I drop my fork. "Maid of *honor*?!!" This is too much.

"Don't talk with your mouth full, Rye," Dad scolds lightly.

I seal up my mouth and chew as quick as possible, my

eyes betraying every emotion I'm having inside. Tears streaming down my face, smile on my mouth. I'm so fucking honored. I swallow and then grab both of their hands. "I won't let you down. I promise."

They both laugh. They know there's no way I ever could.

Chapter 2

Ash

"Dad, I have to leave early today."

"What did I say about calling me 'dad' at the office?" I chuckle as I throw my briefcase down on the sofa in my office and start to remove my coat.

My son, Jarred, follows me inside, brushing his long, dark blonde hair out of his face. "Okay, Mr. Hawthorn, Ashton, or Ash? Which is better?"

"Probably best if you just never refer to me ever," I reply, crossing toward my desk. "You know you don't have to excuse yourself to me. You're the CFO, after all."

Jarred sighs. "You say that, but I know the one day I kick off early, you're going to call an emergency meeting and then give me hell for it later."

"Give you hell? Do I give you hell?" I say with a frown. For being the CEO of a Fortune 500 company, I think I'm pretty tame as a boss.

He looks away from me. "No... "

I laugh. I can still see the little five-year old in him, the one so eager to please. It's one of the perks of working with my sons. Keeps me grounded. Reminds me that everyone around me was once a child and they deserve grace for it. "What do you need to leave early for?"

"Piper's nanny has a migraine, so I'm on pickup duty today," Jarred replies, tightening his hands on the files in his hands.

"You know you can always leave when it comes to Piper." Piper, my granddaughter, my only grandchild. The current love of my life. Never thought I'd love being a grandfather at forty-six, but here I am.

He nods. "I know, I know, just coming up on the end of the first quarter, I want to make sure that we've gone over all the numbers and—"

My office phone goes off, and I hold one finger up to Jarred, asking him for a second as I grab it. "Hello?"

"Clay Linden for you, sir," my secretary says kindly.

"Put him on, thank you," I reply and then say to Jarred, "Have to take this, son."

"I'll leave these here for you to look over," he replies and puts the folders on my desk.

"Thanks," I say, settling into my desk chair. "And, Jarred?"

Jarred turns around with an expectant gaze.

"Don't worry about leaving early. Numbers are numbers. Piper's always more important than numbers."

His face brightens. He beams. Piper has been his everything since her birth. And for a single dad, he's doing a bang-up job. Hopefully, I did a thing or two right in that department for him to learn from.

"Ash?" Clay's voice comes on the phone.

I grin. "Clay, buddy! How are you?"

"Great. How are you doing?"

I touch one of the folders. "You know how end of the quarter is."

Clay grunts. "Don't I ever."

I chuckle. Clay was the CFO of Hawthorn until just a couple years ago when he decided to leave the business sector in favor of learning to *cook*. The guy can make a ratatouille better than Remy the rat. "What do I owe the pleasure of your call?"

"Well, I've asked Giselle to marry me."

My jaw falls. "What?!"

"And she said yes. I should mention that."

"Congratulations, man! Wow," I say with enthusiasm, turning my gaze out the window. My office is situated downtown right by the river. It's a great place to let your mind wander. "How do you feel?"

"Oh, great. I feel really great."

My gut twists. I'm so happy for him, really. But I'm a little jealous. Clay lost his wife and fell right into Giselle only a year later. Mine's been gone over ten now and I haven't even gotten the courage to look at a woman, let alone think about downloading one of those godforsaken apps. "I'm so happy for you, Clay," I say. "Really. You two deserve it."

"I wanted to ask you if you'd be my best man."

The edge of jealousy morphs into gratitude. "Seriously?"

"Of course. You're the reason I was able to... I wouldn't have been able to get through losing Heather without you."

Clay and I spent a lot of nights together after Heather's cancer diagnosis. And when she inevitably passed away, he practically lived with me since his daughter was away at college. I have to admit, it felt good to be able to help someone suffering like I did when I lost Rose. At least something good came out of that tragedy. I was able to help Clay.

He's never stopped letting me know how grateful he is to me. "I'd be honored," I say heartily.

We chat a little bit more about the details. The proposal, simple in Lincoln Park during one of their walks. The date of the wedding, September eighteenth. The honeymoon they're more eager to plan, probably to Japan.

"Listen, my daughter—you remember my daughter, right?"

I frown. Barely, if I'm completely honest. The last time I saw her was probably Heather's funeral. All of twenty years old, losing her mom couldn't have been easy, but she had her friends with her and I was more focused on his grief than hers. I don't think I spared her more than a cursory look, more worried about my friend, honestly. But I answer, "Of course." No need for him to know I can hardly remember her.

"Well, we've tasked her with planning the wedding since Giselle is less than thrilled about all the details," he laughs. "And Rye is talented, you know, she's a florist."

Right. The florist. That's a cute job.

"But she might need a little help. And with her being Giselle's maid of honor and you being my best man—"

"I get it," I chuckle. "Sure. Why not?" Haven't got much better to do with my free time, unless I'm spending it with my family. But they're all busy with their own lives. They don't need to feel beholden to dragging their old dad around.

I can hear Clay smile over the phone. "Great. I owe you."

"You never owe me anything, Clay."

He makes a bashful sound and then gives me the details, "Come by the house Saturday morning. You and

Rye can meet up and head to a couple venues we have organized appointments at."

"You two are really hands off about this, huh? What if we end up giving you the tackiest wedding on the face of the planet?"

"Oh, I don't give a shit what the wedding looks like. Everything could be neon green and there could be a bagpipe player," Clay says and then lets out a dreamy sigh. "As long as Giselle's my wife at the end of the day... that's all I can ask for."

I bite the inside of my cheek. Fuck, that makes me emotional. I remember that feeling when I married Rose. We were just kids. Eighteen. Jarred was already six months old. And it didn't matter that we didn't have a lot of money to make everything beautiful. All that mattered was that we were there, ready to show up for each other for the rest of our lives. That's what makes marriage beautiful.

I know I should be grateful I met the love of my life, even if I lost her prematurely. Love like that only happens once. Clay must be an exception to that rule.

That could never happen to me.

Chapter 3

Rye

"This is... a lot," I say as I look at the list of venues I've scrobbled together. Yes, I was the one in charge of making the list, and *no,* I didn't pay attention to the location. I've got appointments across the city. Bridgeport, Logan Square, Hyde Park... and getting around Chicago can be a pain in the ass, let me tell you.

"What'd you say, sweetie?" Giselle asks, looking up from her computer. She's been working all morning on editing a paper for publication.

I don't want to stress her out more than she already is. Plus, I'm basically the wedding planner. I got this. "Oh, nothing, nothing," I say.

She narrows her eyes from behind her red-rimmed acetate glasses. "I can tell when you're lying, Rye."

"How? That's not fair!" I whine.

Giselle laughs. "I know you too well, Rye."

I can't help but smile. I'm glad she knows me that well. "I just overbooked myself. That's all. I'm going to be trapped on Lake Shore Drive all day."

"Oof. And the construction has been awful southbound," she mutters.

"*Great*," I say and get up to top off my cup of coffee. "Not to mention, I've got like three vendors to call back and I haven't even gotten started on finding a DJ." I stop suddenly. "Or did you want a live band?"

Giselle stands to meet me at the counter. "Honey, you can't put so much pressure on the situation."

I bug out my eyes. "You're getting married, Giselle! Of course, I have to put pressure on the situation. Plus, y'all want to get married in six months and that's like *no* time in the wedding industry."

Her face softens. "You're already a pro at this, I can tell."

"Does being a pro mean having an aneurysm over something? Because I feel close to it," I say with a huff. Ever since Dad and Giselle asked me to take the helm on wedding planning, I've been losing it. It was fun at first, but now it's just details and *planning*.

She touches the back of my neck and squeezes, which calms me down immensely. I don't know how she does it. "The last thing I want is for you to have an aneurysm over my wedding. That'd be absolutely ridiculous."

"I just want it to be perfect. You two deserve that." The doorbell rings. I frown. "Expecting someone?"

"Oh, yes!" Giselle claps her hands together. "It's your assistant!"

I snort. "My what?"

Dad gets to the front door before Giselle and me. I'm still confused out of my mind. Did they hire me an assistant? If so, *that's* ridiculous. They should have just hired a wedding planner at that point. I lean up against the doorframe into the kitchen and wait, just like I did when I was a little kid so I could see who was coming and still have the ability to duck away if I had to. That's totally appropriate behavior for a nearly thirty-year-old woman, right?

As soon as Dad opens the door, my jaw drops. No fucking way. It can't be.

Ashton Hawthorn is at the front door. I haven't seen this man in years, but he's haunted me all that time. And, fuck, he still looks great. His dark hair swooped back, hair graying at the temples in such a wonderful, delicious way. Scruff peppers his jaw that is so sharp it could cut you like glass. And his dark green eyes, as pristine and endless as emeralds, radiate just as intensely as I remember.

He probably doesn't even remember me. That's the kicker. I have obsessed over this man since I was sixteen years old for no other reason than... than...

He's fucking perfect.

"Ash!" my dad cries out and pulls his friend into a hug. My dad's not a short man but looks like a dwarf next to Ashton who towers above him.

Ash grins and pats my dad on the back before moving onto Giselle. "Look at you two. You're both glowing," he says, beaming, his white teeth sending an electric shock through my spine.

"You're a flatterer, Ashton," Giselle says and then gives him kisses on both cheeks.

They usher Ash into the front hall. I resist every urge to dart back into the kitchen and hide behind the island. I have to face him.

My stomach drops when I remember what Giselle said when the doorbell rang: *your assistant.*

No. Fucking. Way.

Chapter 4

Ash

I've been in the front hall of Clay's house more times than I can count over the years. The greeting is always the same, jovial and friendly. We're close enough that I usually just show myself in, go plop down on one of the leather easy chairs in the den or grab a beer from the kitchen.

But today, I'm stuck in place because there's a new face in the front hall. Someone I don't recognize. And she's... stunning. With miles of dark chocolate hair flowing down her shoulders and eyes as blue as the ocean, this woman looks like an oasis. The curves of her body look plush, from her lips to her waist to her thighs. I could devour her.

What the fuck is happening? I haven't had such an immediate attraction to someone in years. It's a feeling deep in my gut. Inevitable. Primal. I want her so bad; I almost think I can smell her.

"You remember Rye, don't you?" Clay pipes up.

Rye??? That's not Rye. Rye is still a little girl. Isn't she? There's no way that the shy and aloof girl that hung around in the kitchen doorway to say a polite hello is this beautiful woman standing in the front hall. This must be a joke.

"Good to see you again, Mr. Hawthorn," the woman says, cocking her head to the side and smiling in such a way that I think I could faint.

It *is* her. Shit. I've just sexualized my best friend's daughter to absolute filth. I guess to be fair to myself, I didn't recognize her, but I probably *should* have recognized her. Dear god, I am having heart palpitations.

I try to smile, lips twitching, blinking too much. "Wow, it's been... you've really grown up."

"Don't remind me," Clay groans and wraps his arm around Rye's shoulder. "She's still my little girl."

I think I need to go throw up. Purge this feeling as soon as possible.

"Dad, please don't do this," Rye says with a sheepish smile.

"Thank you so much for helping Rye out with the planning, Ash," Giselle says with a hand on my bicep. "It's good to have an outside eye, I think."

Maybe I can back out. Get through today and then, surprise! My company is suffering and I need to put all my attention into that. Or whoops! Totally forgot that I have to shine my shoes! Yeah, there's no good reason for me to back out of this, especially when Clay is my best friend in the whole world. "Don't mention it," I say, slipping my hands into the pockets of my light wool coat. "You said venues today."

"Yep! Rye already did all the leg work and she has a list right here. You can drive her."

"Giselle... " Rye says warily. "I don't want to make him chauffeur me."

"Nonsense," I say eagerly. That'll give me a good

distraction. Have to keep my eyes on the road. *Not* on the beautiful woman who turns out to be my best friend's adult daughter who I want to ravage completely and utterly and cannot and *will not ever do that*. "I'm happy to drive."

If I were my usual self, I might make a witty joke, offer a little flirtation or something. But I've got to keep a cold front.

Clay squeezes Rye to his chest. "His car is nicer anyway."

Rye blushes. "I like my Nissan. It's sturdy. Hardy. You know." She turns her gaze to me. "For potholes and things."

I suck in my lower lip. Not responding. Not interested. Although I feel bad when she looks away, feeling rejected. I wish I could just be nice, but I can't because being nice leads to being... friendly and friendliness can get you in a world of trouble.

"Well, today, you'll ride in style," Clay says, nodding to me.

"Yep," I say.

Rye checks her phone. "Well, we better go. We have an appointment at the Historical Society in twenty." She rushes to the hall tree to grab a light blue jacket that hangs open, still giving me a clear view of her beautiful body. *Great*.

"Take good care of her, Ash," Giselle says. Fuck, is she a mind reader? "No speeding."

Right, the car. "Don't worry. Twenty-five miles per hour, *tops*."

Rye giggles. No. No giggling. I can't make her laugh. That's going to tip the scale too much. I watch Rye say goodbye to Clay and Giselle; I give them a parting wave before opening the front door for Rye. As she brushes past me, she whispers a thank you, and I get a whiff of her hair that smells like a beach house in Cape Cod. Salty and sweet at once with an undercurrent of some sort of flower I can't identify. Makes my brain soft.

I open the car doors from my phone, the falcon wings of the car rising up. Rye stops short and stares. I try not to chuckle. It's not like she hasn't grown up around money. Perhaps all the time in... where was she? Iowa? Wisconsin? Perhaps she got used to simpler things.

"They won't hit you," I say, rounding the car to the driver's seat. "They've got sensors."

"Jeez. That's intense," she says and sinks into the passenger seat carefully, pulling her limbs and purse as close to her body as possible as the doors shut.

As soon as we're situated, I drive off down the street and head to the Historical Society on Clark. We are both quiet, and the lack of music playing on the radio doesn't help the situation.

"Thank you for driving," Rye speaks softly.

"No problem," I say, trying to harden my face as much as possible. My eyes are so focused on the road they might as well not be seeing anything at all. I grip the steering wheel tight and try not to think about how close she is to me. But apparently, I can't send that message down to my dick because I'm half-hard.

Rye is quiet, watching the world go by. "Feels weird to be back."

I know I should reply. I just can't. I am repeating in my head *Don't be hard, don't be hard, don't be hard.* This isn't an effective method to getting rid of an erection.

"So, how are your kids? Three boys, right?"

I soften when she asks this. The distraction does wonders for the blood rushing to my crotch. "Yep. Three boys. All grown up now, though," I say, unable to contain a small smile. "They all work with me."

"That must be nice," she says. I can feel her eyes on me, prying me for more. "I think I'm the same age as your eldest."

"Jarred? He's twenty-nine."

"Yeah. Me too."

I breathe a sigh of relief. At least she's not a baby. I'm not a total perv for thinking she's a beautiful woman. I should have been able to do that math in my head. I'm just too hopped up on testosterone to think straight.

Before she can say another word, I turn on the radio and turn up the volume. A little louder than I normally would. Just loud enough to send the message that there's no need for conversation. Perhaps I'm being cruel. Unkind. But it'd be way worse to cross this line. I can deal with being the bad guy if that means I'm protecting us all from a situation we could never come back from.

Chapter 5

Rye

The Chicago History Museum is a no, and the Bridgeport Arts Center is a maybe. Now we're at a little place in Logan Square, a building right on Kedzie that looks unassuming enough until you step inside of a little piece of heavenly history.

Things have been awkward. Tense even. I don't know how to describe it. Ash is not the affable man I remember him being. Something seems to be on his mind. That, or he's just turned into an asshole in the past nine years. Every time I try to make small talk, he only gives me single-word answers. The only time he initiated a conversation with me was to ask if I was cold and if he should turn up the heat (I wasn't so he didn't).

I think it might have something to do with me. Maybe he can smell my desire for him and is trying to make it known that it will never happen. Because with both of the people giving us walkthroughs of the venues, he's been charming and friendly. He's even asked questions and remarked on how lovely certain things are.

Why is he a block of ice to me?

As we walk inside of the last venue of the day, I nearly trip over my own feet. That or there's a fold in the carpet. Ash grabs me by the elbow to steady me and I feel electricity zip through my body. "You alright?"

I look up at him with wide eyes and swallow. "Yeah. Thank you."

He releases my arm without another word, turning away from me as if I'm just a crack in the pavement. Jesus, if he's going to act like this, I think I'd rather plan the whole wedding myself and deal with the aforementioned aneurysm.

"Ms. Linden?" a woman with a dark pageboy cut appears from the hallway and greets us with a big smile.

"That's me!" I say, my voice a bit sweeter and higher-pitched than it usually is.

"Great to meet you. Is this your fiancé?" she asks, turning to Ash.

I think I turn as white as a sheet. "Uhm, uh, no, no. This is—"

"Family friend," Ash answers smoothly with a slick smile.

"I'm looking—It's not my wedding," I say with nervous laughter between my words. The implication that I'm getting married is shocking enough, let alone the implication I'd be marrying *Ashton Hawthorn.* "My dad. And his girlfriend. I'm here on their behalf."

The woman blinks and then smiles apologetically, "I'm so sorry. You did say that on the phone. Forgive me."

I wave my hand. "No apology necessary."

Ash clears his throat suddenly. "Anyway, could you show us the space?" What is with this guy? Does he have somewhere to be? Because I think I'd rather him be there than here with this attitude.

"Right this way."

She leads us through the building to an old elevator. When it arrives, we have to open a gate to get inside. We squeeze inside and as soon as the gate closes and the elevator heaves up underneath us, I realize how close I am to Ash. I'm facing him right at chest level. I can smell his cologne. Expensive... but clean. Uncomplicated. He's holding his face tight, no doubt thinking I'm way too close to him. His dimples are tighter than usual. Why does he hate me?

Even though he's being an asshole, I still can't resist the thought of him. What would my lips feel like grazed up against the scruff on his neck? Would his Adam's apple bob nervously with my hand on his chest? It's so wrong to imagine it. I've thought as much ever since I was sixteen and he started appearing in my dreams. But it makes it taste a little bit better knowing how wrong and taboo it would be if we actually...

"Here we are!" the woman, Dani, announces and leads us out of the elevator.

Ash couldn't move faster away from me, briskly following her down the hall. I sigh and trail behind them having to simmer in these fantasies I wish I didn't have.

Luckily, the venue makes up for the awkward elevator ride. It's a beautiful ballroom with gilded ceilings. Perfect for the reception. As Dani explains all the amenities and suggest setups, I can see it all playing out before me. I can picture Giselle and my dad embracing and laughing as they trip across the dance floor.

"Wow, this is lovely," I say.

"I'm glad you think so. It's perfect for the semi-intimate wedding you spoke about on the phone. You can have a long guest list, but the venue gives it a more personal feel," Dani expresses, gesturing to the room with her hands. "It's also incredibly versatile. Like a canvas. Depending on the vendors you choose and the décor, you can really make this place feel exactly how you want."

I smile to myself.

"Could you draw up a contract now?" Ash speaks suddenly.

I shoot him a look. We haven't even discussed it, and *yes,* I do feel good about it, but I should have at least had a say.

I'm grateful Dani looks at me for confirmation before she responds. "Absolutely. Follow me to my office."

We go to the office and get the paperwork drawn up. Ash says he's going to take it home with him and look it over tonight. He'll send it over in the morning should he find everything agreeable. The way he's talking is as if this is a business merger and not a wedding.

Of course, I'm nothing but pleasant on our way out of the venue, thanking Dani profusely. But as Ash and I walk in silence back to his car, the frustration that has been brewing throughout the day is now almost spilling out. I can only sit in so many awkward silences, only let him get away with being a demanding businessman a few times before I'm annoyed.

"I'm taking you home now, right?" Ash says in a gruff voice.

"Right. Thanks," I say. I chew on my lower lip trying to hold back, but it's no use. Attraction be damned. If we're going to plan this wedding together, something's got to give. "That's a nice space."

Ash flips on his turn signal, eyes scanning the road. "I think so."

"Is that why you asked for a contract without consulting me?"

His eyebrows jump up slightly. I've taken him off-guard. And his silence makes me worry I've made him angry. "I... it seemed that you liked it."

"Well, yes. I did. But I'd like you to at least ask me next time."

"Noted."

"After all, it's my dad's wedding."

"Right. And I'm doing your dad a favor by helping you with all of this, so forgive me if I don't want to be schlepping around the venues next Saturday too," he says scathingly.

I scoff. "Well, if you feel like this favor is more trouble than it's worth, I'd prefer to do all of this on my own." That couldn't be farther from the truth. I want help. I *need* help. And to be honest, the way he dealt with the contract and everything is something I can learn from. We need to get on the same page, some baseline of respect and communication.

He looks askance to me, his forest green eyes taking my breath away. Fuck, why doesn't my brain equate jerk to unattractive?

"I'm sorry, I didn't mean to imply... " he trails off and swallows. "I'm happy to do this for Clay. For your dad."

Then act like it.

"I've just got a lot on my mind. But that doesn't excuse how I've treated you or—" Ash shakes his head, clearing the slate of his thoughts. "I hope you can forgive me, Rye."

I play with the zipper of my purse in my lap. When he says that, I am struck with how painful it's been to be treated with coldness by the only man that I've ever really felt something for. Even though it's ridiculous, even though we've never so much as even touched or flirted. He's captivated me all this time, a lighthouse I am always trying to get back to and yet I'm stuck in the current of waves that is my life, bound to never get to him. "It's alright. I've got a lot on my mind too," I say. It's the truth. I just won't tell him that he's the one taking up my brain space.

Ash's lips perk into a smile. I swear it's the first one he's given me since we left the house this morning. "At least give me one more shot to be a better assistant, huh?"

When it comes to me, Ash can have a hundred more shots. I'll let him try and try and try as long as I get to be around him. Even if he's a jerk. "One more shot," I say with a cheeky smile.

* * *

"Ash? Your dad is having you work with *Ash*?"

"I know."

"But he's –"

"I *know*."

I'm talking with my friend Dara on the phone as I take a walk down Armitage Avenue. I left her behind when I left Madison. We met a couple years ago when she worked at the bakery near the flower shop. We were immediately kindred spirits, the type of friends you only come across once in a while. Soon after, she was my best friend. We've talked every day since I've left. She was more excited than I was about the wedding planning.

"This is so exciting, Rye."

I frown. "This isn't exciting. This is terrible."

"But Rye...you *like* him."

Dara knows about the desperate, years-long crush I've had on him. She's always been weirdly reassuring me that one day it *will* happen. It's the romantic in her.

"What if this is the first step in you two actually –"

"*Don't*. Do *not*," I say firmly. "It's not going to happen."

"But –"

"Dara!"

"Rye!"

"Do you know what that would do to my dad? He would fucking freak. The guy's his best friend," I say. I've thought about it over and over in my head. When I first developed the crush at sixteen, it was just that. A crush. The fact Ash was my dad's best friend was just a minor detail. But as I've gotten older and lived more life, I found that's simply *not* a minor detail. And besides. It'll never happen. "It doesn't matter. He hates me anyway."

Dara snorts, the sound slamming into my eardrum. "There's no way."

"Um. Yeah. Yeah, there is," I reply, thinking about the day we just spent together. "I don't know. He was rude the entire time. And we barely talked. I was too... nervous."

"Of course you were. He's your crush."

"*Dara...*"

She sighs. "Listen, Rye. It's the first day. You two are going to be spending months planning this wedding together. It will get better."

I stop at a crosswalk and wait for a car to pass. Will it get better? I'm not too sure. "He was really cold. I don't know. It was like I did something wrong."

"You're too hard on yourself, baby. You'll get around it. Trust me. You're too wonderful to be rude to forever," she says sweetly.

There's trusty old Dara. I keep her around for a reason. She's as sweet as pie, and it's not just because she's a baker. "You're the best, Dar."

"Aw, shucks. I'm just saying what's true."

I smile to myself and turn down my street.

"*And*... just be open. You never know what could happen."

I grimace. "Girl, it's not going to happen."

"I didn't say anything specific," she says defensively. "I just said... you never know."

I laugh. I know exactly what she's dancing around. "Okay, Dara. You're right. Who knows what will happen."

I might not know exactly what the future holds for me and Ash, but I know one thing.

It doesn't include anything to do with that sticky, molassesy crush. That is something I'll keep tucked away because it can never, ever come out.

Chapter 6

Ash

I tiptoe down the hallway carefully toward the hall closet. It's open just an inch. A suspiciously good hiding spot for a little girl.

"Where's Piper?" I ask expressively. "She's really stumped me this time..." I put my hand around the door knob. "I hope I haven't lost her."

I hear a giggle from inside the closet. Bingo.

"What will I tell her daddy if I can't find –" I throw open the door and find little Piper Hawthorn sitting on top of a pile of shoes in the closet, wearing a jolly little grin. "Gotcha!"

Piper laughs loudly and leaps into my arms. "You found me!"

"Thank goodness! I was scared I'd never see you again!" I announce, sniffling melodramatically. "Who would I give all my kisses to?" I start to kiss Piper's cheeks and neck over and over, quick pecks.

She wraps her arms tighter around me. She's so tiny, even at three years old. But I can tell she's getting bigger. Sooner than I even know, I'm not going to be able to pick her up. I've got to take every moment I can. "Now *you* hide, Grampa!"

"Now listen," I say and start to carry her back down the hall to the dining room where I hear an eager throng of voices. "I love playing hide and seek with you, honey, but I know everyone else would love to spend some time with you too."

Piper grunts. "Can I sit on your lap?"

"Of course. I have a perfect Piper-sized space for you."

She hums contentedly and rests her head on my shoulder. I've missed having little ones around. My kids have been grown up for a while now. And while my pride wasn't thrilled to be a grandfather at such a young age, Piper's the best thing that's happened to me since... well, since Rose passed away. I can see so much of Rose in her, just in her light brown hair. They would have loved each other.

I walk into the dining room with Piper on my hip to my favorite sight: my family. And then some. The boys and I have been having weekly Sunday night dinners for years now. And while it started out as just the four of us, we've collected people along the way.

The first was Juniper Reed, or June as we all call her, Keifer's best friend since kindergarten. While she's always been a part of the family, she's really fit right in since her parents left town. Us Hawthorns have become her home base. They're currently sitting at the head of the table going through Keifer's Tinder together. I'm way past the point of giving them shit for being a man and a woman and being best friends. I've never seen a more platonic pair.

"You've only swiped right on blondes," June says, side-eyeing Keifer.

"That's not true!"

June snorts, jabbing her elbow into his side. "Just admit you have a type!"

Keifer slumps down in his chair and brings the phone closer to his face. "I don't want your help. You're rude."

"Just give this to me! Let me swipe!"

Those two always make me smile.

Some years later, we collected Trevor McCoy, Oliver's best friend from their time at DePaul together. All my boys went to school close to home. Northwestern, University of Chicago, DePaul. But Trevor's from California. Freshman year, he wasn't able to fly home for Thanksgiving, so he joined us and never stopped. He works in the business sector too, but on the investing side of things. We tend not to talk shop. It's a rule we leave work at the door... for the most part. But that's easy with Trevor, because he's like a golden retriever type of guy in all ways, save his jet-black hair. Always smiling and cracking jokes. I love him like a son because of how much he's brought Oliver out of his shell. Oliver got very serious after losing Rose, and I was worrying his guardedness was getting in his way. Then he met Trevor. Thank God.

They're currently arguing over DND classes with a vehemence seen only in most television courtrooms.

"Wood elves are the better elf," Oliver announces. "I don't care what you say."

"Are you kidding? The spellcasting abilities of high elves makes them vastly superior," Trevor scoffs.

Oliver rolls his eyes. "That's exactly what a 'high' elf would say. Pretentious ass..."

"Guys, guys!" the woman between them cries out, holding her hands up as if separating a fight. That's Rowan. Trevor's girlfriend of about a year. The newest addition to our Sunday night dinners. Only between

Trevor and Oliver in the literal sense. Otherwise, the three of them have become a triumvirate, especially with all their rather nerdy activities. They're in a DND group together, go to conventions together, and even went as Mario, Luigi, and Princess Peach for Halloween last year. Dark-haired and gray-eyed, I knew when I saw her she's the type of woman who takes no shit. "Drow is *obviously* the best kind of elf for darkvision *alone*. I'm not taking questions."

"The lady has spoken," Trevor says, giving Rowan a kiss to the side of her head.

It's nice to have some young love around, especially when my own sons haven't had much of that lately. Not that I'm judging. I know how hard love is to come by. True love. There's a lot of fake love out there, but true, soulmate love, now that's the goal.

I lucked out finding mine so early. I just wish I hadn't lost her so early too.

"Daddy, Daddy, Daddy!" Piper bounces in my arms and starts to strain toward Jarred who is sitting at the table on his own, lost in thought. As per usual.

His concentration breaks and his face softens with a smile. "Piper, Piper, Piper!"

"Wow, ditching me for your dad, huh?" I tease Piper as I hand her over to Jarred and then take a seat in my spot at the head of the table. "I get who your favorite is now."

Piper cuddles up to Jarred but gives me a pouty look. "You're my favorite Grampa and Daddy's my favorite daddy."

I sigh. "I'll take it."

Jarred kisses the top of Piper's head as she sleepily nudges her head into his neck. "So, how was yesterday?"

"Um. Good. It was good."

Oliver leans over from his conversation. "What was yesterday?"

I clear my throat. I have purposefully avoided this topic all night. The only reason Jarred knows is because I babysat Piper Friday night so he could go see a flick with some friends. He asked me what my Saturday looked like and I told him the innocent truth that I was going to help Clay's daughter look at wedding venues. At least it was an innocent truth then.

"Dad's helping plan a wedding," Jarred says excitedly.

"What?! Whose?" Oliver asks.

"Well, let's be clear, I'm the best man in Clay's wedding," I start to correct, but am quickly interrupted again by my youngest son.

"Clay's getting married?" Keifer exclaims.

I reply, "Yes, and he's asked me to be his best man and–"

"Well, congratulations, Mr. H!" Trevor exclaims. He's never gotten over the calling me Mr. H thing, even though I've corrected him a million times.

"Thank you, Trevor," I say and then clear my throat. "And he's asked me to help his daughter, she's the maid of honor–"

Oliver interrupts again, "Aren't the best man and the maid of honor supposed to be like a couple?"

Rowan bats him on the arm. "No, weirdo. What romcom put that idea into your head?"

I swallow and let their argument play out. I'm certainly not in a couple with Clay's daughter. But I am thinking about her and I really wish I wasn't. "*Anyway*," I say loud enough to get the table to quiet down. "I told him I'd help out. So, I am."

"They went to look at wedding venues yesterday," Jarred adds, definitely thinking he's being helpful.

June gasps. "Oh! Where did you look? Where is it going to be?"

"June, relax," Keif scolds her.

"Sorry, I just love weddings," she gushes with an apologetic look to me.

I chuckle. "A mansion down in Logan Park. We decided. Or she did–well, I'm just there to give her assistance. She's a florist, you know, and she's just moved back home, so she's looking at starting a whole new part of her career here. And I've had a wedding. A long time ago. Been to a lot of weddings. So–"

"So have I, and I wouldn't know the first thing about planning one," Jarred says.

I nod and then scan the table. All eyes are on me. This is how it often goes at these dinners. All the kids chattering about their lives with each other, boldly and brashly, me in the background. Until I'm not. "You'd probably be better at it than you think," I say to him and then add, "Besides, Clay's my best friend. I've seen him through his whole relationship with Giselle. Maybe I don't know how to plan weddings, but I have some ideas about how to plan *their* wedding. And between me and Rye, I think we'll make it pretty beautiful." I'm not sure if I believe my own optimism, but I'm sticking with it.

"Jeez, Mr. H," Rowan pipes up, a catlike smile on her face. "I didn't know you were such a romantic."

I bristle at that description. "No, just a good friend, hopefully."

Yes. A good friend. A good friend who helps to plan his friend's wedding and definitely, definitely doesn't think his daughter is even remotely attractive. I'm very hopeful about that.

* * *

"If we cancel the contract, then all of our shipments are going to be delayed for at least the next two weeks," Keifer's voice comes through the car speaker.

"But if legal counseled us to get *out* of the contract, I want to do that ASAP," I say aggravatedly, running a hand over my face.

We've been going back and forth about this issue for about twenty minutes now. I've been parked in front of the flower shop I'm supposed to meet Rye at on my lunch and I've eaten up most of the time dealing with another fucking hiccup at work. Keifer, my youngest son, is usually pretty level-headed which makes him a great Chief Of Operations. He can problem solve almost anything.

But he's still got to report to me. And one of the drawbacks of being your kids' boss is that they think they can talk back.

"We're on thin ice with Truman. We could lose the account."

"Then we'll lose it," I say gruffly. "They can halt their production even trying to lock in a contract with someone else and wait for us to get all of our equipment they're leasing out of there." Ah, the joys of industrial machinery. The glamor.

I peer out my car window. Rye had me meet her at a flower wholesaler on the west side. I'm never out this way. The unassuming warehouse looks like it should be a fulfillment center, not a place for flowers.

"Hello? Are you still there?"

"Cancel the shipping contract. Period. I have a meeting."

Keifer grunts in frustration and hangs up the call. I

always feel like I should say 'I love you' at the end of a work call with my boys, but I've accidentally said it one too many times to my clients that I've had to strip it from my work call vocabulary.

I jump out of the car and rush inside. I'm hit with the sweet aroma of flora. It's potent and fresh and intoxicating. After getting turned around and having to be chaperoned in by one of the workers, I make it into the big greenhouse where there are flats and flats of flowers as far as the eye can see. I don't even know what I'm looking at. It's like someone has managed to bottle up a field of wildflowers. Stunning.

But not nearly as stunning as Rye, who I catch sight of down one of the aisles of flowers, accompanied by an older gentleman with a shock of white hair. I was hoping the time away from her would clear my head. Unfortunately, that is not the case. She's wearing a flowy blouse tucked into some jeans, her hair tied back out of her face so she can observe the flowers without her hair getting in the way. I watch her bend down and take a sniff of some purple flowers and she smiles at the man accompanying her.

I can tame my desire. I really think I can. It's only six months. I don't have to be an asshole. I know plenty of beautiful women who I don't sleep with. Rye could be a perfect example of this. I can live on a fantasy of her if I have to. It'll be over in the blink of an eye. I just need to keep a level head.

I walk down the gravel lane toward the pair, and as I get closer, they both look at me expectantly. "Sorry, I'm late."

"I almost thought you weren't coming," Rye says, almost as if she would have been relieved had I not come at all. Her blue eyes are lined crisply and smoked out with eyeshadow. She doesn't even have to try to give me bedroom eyes. They're just implicit.

The older man does not look pleased that I'm here. I bet he expected to be able to take advantage of Rye by sticking her with an absolutely ludicrous estimate for the flowers. She wouldn't know better, probably.

"I'm sorry," I say again, and I mean it. "Work stuff." Rye is used to this. After all, her dad and I worked together. She knows how intense things can get.

She smiles, and I swear I feel faint. Her glossy lips are coy and sweet. "It's okay, Ash. Don't worry about it."

"These flowers are... nice," I say. I'm not sure what to say. "Pretty." I'm making it worse. I've only paid attention to flowers when I've given them to someone. To Rose. Ironically, she hated receiving roses. Now, I make sure that her headstone is always adorned with some arrangement. But these flowers are all waiting, yearning to find their bouquet, their home. That's sort of beautiful. I'll leave all of this to Rye. Whatever she says, goes. Whatever she wants, I'll do.

That is a very dangerous place to be with a woman.

We weave in and out of the aisles as the man points out different flowers and varietals. Annuals, perennials, et cetera, et cetera. I'm lost in all of this, but Rye is right there with him, nodding and asking questions I wouldn't have ever had even an inkling to ask. I always love watching people in their element. There's a glint in her eye as she scans the rows of flowers. She knows what she's doing. And she's confident. And confidence is...

Come on, Ash. Stop thinking with your dick.

"So, what are we thinking?" he asks in a haggard voice as if he'd like to be anywhere else but here. "September wedding. Peonies will be out of season."

Rye laughs. "People love their peonies, don't they?"

The stoic old man cracks a little smile.

"So, if we stick with the dahlias and hydrangeas as the

statement flowers and work in some Japanese anemone and then use yarrow as filler, what do you think we're looking at price wise?" Rye asks as we stop in front of a patch of greenery that hasn't yet bloomed.

"I'll have to run the numbers. And it depends on how many arrangements you want made."

"Well, I'll be arranging them, so I can give you the specs on that."

He frowns. "Are you sure you want to do that?"

Rye raises an eyebrow. "I'm sorry?"

"I mean, that's a lot of work if you don't know what you're doing."

"Well, I'm a florist."

"Yeah, but bouquets and events are completely different animals, little lady."

He hasn't bothered to learn her name, that's certain. I can't stand his tone. The condescending, infantilizing way he's speaking to her. I've never understood how so many men think they can get away with that kind of behavior.

"I think I'll be just fine," Rye says, still smiling. She's holding her hands in front of her, twisting one of the rings on her finger nervously.

"How about I show you what some of your contractors can do and then you won't even have to have that on your plate, hm?" he presses and touches her back.

I know this game. He definitely gets a payout when contractors get clients. His sales technique is as transparent as glass.

"I think she's made it clear she's going to do the arrangements," I say without thinking.

Rye looks to me wide-eyed, her blue eyes wavering. Shit, I think I've made her angry. She can handle herself,

I'm sure. She doesn't need me defending her. But I can't stand this guy's tactics.

The older man looks to me, that annoyance that was in his face earlier even more obvious.

"She's more than capable. Has she shown you her stuff?" I add with a smile. Play the dumb, friendly fool. Always works. "I'm more than confident that she knows what she's doing. In fact—" I reach into my pocket and pull out my wallet to slide out my black Amex. "I'll take a bunch of those... those... and those... " I point around to various flowers that have caught my eye. "So, she can start planning in the meantime."

"Ash, you don't have to do that," Rye mutters, but the man has slipped the card out of my hand before there's any room to change either of our minds.

We follow him into the front office to complete the transaction. We arrange for the flowers to be delivered to the Linden house. They're going to have hyacinths bursting out the windows for days. Rye is silent the entire interaction until we say goodbye. I've fucked up. Somehow, after the boorish way I acted when we were venue hunting, I've made it even worse. I think I need to bow out. And if that means Clay needs to find a new best man, so be it.

It's misting outside when we exit the warehouse. Classic turn of March into April in Chicago. "Listen, Rye, I didn't mean—"

"Oh my god, that was amazing," she says simultaneously with a broad grin.

I stare at her.

"Did you see the look on his face? And then when you pulled out your credit card? God!" She lets out a ream of laughter and claps her hands together. "That was priceless!"

I laugh sheepishly, so glad I've read her wrong.

"Although, seriously, you did not have to buy all those flowers. I'll have dad pay you back," she says, pushing her hands into her pockets.

"No, no," I say adamantly. It's barely a drop in the bucket for me, but I don't want to say this. Even though I'm easily classified in the one percent, it's not something I like to talk about. It's tacky. "Consider it a peace offering for how I acted last time."

Rye waves her hand. "Seriously, Ash, it's not a big deal."

"But it is. I knew you when you were a kid, Rye." I get a nauseous feeling. I knew her when she was *a kid*. I should admire her beauty with awe that she's grown up so much. Not because I want every part of her. "I want you to feel safe with me."

Rye flushes. "I do."

We're standing about a foot apart facing each other. There's a pull I feel inside my belly, a magnetism toward her. And for the slightest moment, it looks like she has it too. Are we going to hug? Even that would be too much.

Rye pulls her car keys out of her coat pocket and starts to back away. That was a close call. "Thanks, Ash. See you next weekend for the DJ?"

"Sounds good. See you then."

As she walks away, I notice a spring in her step. Her long brown hair swings from side to side with her hips.

She is a beautiful girl. And I will be in awe of her. Distant. Impersonal.

Some man will be so lucky to have her. And I have no idea how to feel about that.

Chapter 7

Rye

"You doing alright?"

I look over at my dad. "Yeah. Why?"

"You're doing that thing with your necklace."

I realize my fingers are on the circular metal pendant around my neck. My mother's. I've worn it ever since she passed away. When I'm nervous, I pull it back and forth across the chain. Sometimes, I don't even realize I'm doing it. I drop my hand from the necklace and laugh lightly. "Oh, I don't know. Just don't want to be late."

"It's still ten minutes before he's supposed to pick you up, isn't it?"

I swallow. I've been standing in the front window, waiting, like I'm a little girl waiting for Santa Claus to come. I've been ready for a half hour already. I have no other way to pass the time than to wait because my mind is consumed with Ash.

Ever since he helped me with the flowers, my feelings have returned with a vengeance. I can't sleep without dreaming of him.

Dad comes up behind me and smooths his hands over my shoulders. "Just relax."

"I want this to be perfect for you," I say with a smile. It's always an easy excuse to pin my emotions on the wedding. I do want it to be perfect.

"Rye, it *will* be perfect. Just the fact you and Ash are putting so much effort into making the day special makes it perfect."

I sigh. Yes. Ash and me. Working together to make it special. My dad's marriage to Giselle will always come with the memories and reminders of my stupid schoolgirl crush.

It's not stupid, though. That's what my therapist has had to remind me. It's not stupid because my feelings are real. The longer I spend making myself feel stupid for wanting a man I met as a kid, the harder it will be to move on from the feelings.

"And there he is. Early," Dad says, gesturing out the window to Ash's gunmetal ride that's just pulled up outside.

My heart flutters and I repeat in my head:

It's not stupid, it's not stupid, it's not stupid.

* * *

"I'm sorry. You specialize in... ?" Ash trails off.

"Disco. And funk," the band leader, DJ, as he's called, says with a toothy smile. "We bring DeFUNK. Get it?"

DeFUNK. I should have known from the name of the band.

"Uh-hm... " Ash says, looking askance to me.

I had no idea when I arranged this meeting that this was a disco band. I didn't even know there were such things this day and age, but shows you what I know. There's a market for everything. I had just gone through the top ten highest reviewed wedding bands on Yelp and organized meetings with all of those available for the wedding date.

DeFUNK was number ten. I should have known something was up then and there.

"Listen, man, I'll pay you for your time, but I don't know if disco is really—"

"I know what you're thinking. Disco? At a wedding? Sounds wrong. But there's no music more grooving and more danceable than disco. If you want your guests up out of their seats and dancing until their feet fall off, then we're the band for you. You bring the dancers, we bring DeFUNK."

I sigh and murmur, "Oh my god, he has a catchphrase."

Ash chuckles. "What do you think? Should we give him a chance?"

"You know what? We're here, you're here. What the hell. Show us what you got," I say with a smile.

Things today have been good. Ash and I have interviewed four other bands. They've brought their A-game. All of them are super talented, so I don't yet feel a call in any direction.

Ash, however, apparently has very discerning taste when it comes to music for the wedding. The first band is out because their singer was a raspy coffee house cover kind of girl and the third was out because they featured a banjo. I'm shocked he's even willing to give DeFUNK a go.

DJ goes to strike up the band, counting them in from the bass drum. They are all dressed in disco adjacent clothing. He forewarned us that they go *all out* when it comes to performances, so this is just a little taste. "The La Croix of stage clothes."

They launch into a song I can only describe as *funky.*

Just as he described. The groove is intense, the woman playing bass guitar leading smoothly.

"Parliament. Nice," Ash murmurs to himself.

"You're into DeFUNK, Ash?" I ask.

If he says "no," I know he's lying. He's tapping his foot and bobbing his head along.

"They weren't wrong, it does make you want to get up and dance."

I smile. "You like to dance, Ash?"

"Only by myself in my bedroom."

I get a flash in my head of Ash grooving to this song. Probably naked. I feel hot around the collar. "You wanna show me some moves?" I ask.

"God, no," he says with an askew smile.

The band looks like they're having so much fun. I get it now. Who cares about the reputation of disco and funk? This fucking rocks.

"What if I dance first?" I say, getting out of my seat and starting a little toe tap side to side. "Would you join me?"

Ash looks at me like I'm crazy before letting out a loud laugh. "Seriously?"

It's hard not to feel this kind of music in your bones. The beat just informs every part of me and gets my hips swaying side to side.

"Don't leave her hanging, man!" DJ shouts out mid-song from behind the set.

The band encourages me to keep going and the peer pressure is enough to get Ash out of his seat. His mouth forms a tight line and he touches the button on the front of his gray suit jacket. When he picked me up this morning, I had to keep myself from gasping. What on earth was he doing so dressed up on a *Saturday*? Gray suit with a white dress shirt underneath unbuttoned just enough to reveal the beginning of his dark chest hair and a red pocket square. Divine...

He does his best to start on a rhythmic pattern of stepping side to side. And for a guy who only dances in his bedroom alone, he's got some moves. I can imagine with a drink or two in him, he'd let way, way loose. I'd like to see it.

This is why Ash has remained foremost on my mind ever since I was a girl. There's just something about him. He's intoxicated me. He's been my drug. I've lived off memories of him. Yearned and pined. Even when I've been in relationships or dated guys, he's always there in my mind.

It's tragic. It's depressing. It's pathetic. And he can *never, ever know*.

Now, facing one another, we boogie. That's the best way to describe it. We boogie! It feels good.

"Okay, Rye Linden, you've got some moves!" Ash announces over the throbbing bass guitar.

"So do you! Why are you saving them for the bedroom?" I ask and then immediately realize how suggestive that sounds. "I mean—"

Ash laughs loudly, throwing his head back. "Don't worry, I know what you meant, Rye."

I laugh too, although it sounds more like a bird dying because I'm so stressed, and now I'm thinking about what moves he does have. Is he a breasts or ass guy? Does he like to take a girl from behind or does he want to look her in the eyes? What are his kinks?

I'm wet. I'm dancing to funk music with Ashton Hawthorn and I'm wet.

His hair is somehow sweaty. How hard are we dancing? A lock of it falls heavily onto his forehead and he pushes it back with his broad hand. Fuck, I'm spiraling out of control.

"I have to use the bathroom," I suddenly chirp and rush

out of the room to find the bathroom. Ash calls after me, but I ignore him.

I manage to find it after stumbling down the hall and trying every door that I see. Desperate. I'm so desperate to get this energy out. I lock the door behind me and immediately unzip my jeans so I can fit my hand into my crotch and...

My breath seizes as my fingers glide across my clit. So wet. How can I be so wet? Nothing has even happened. It's the curse of an active imagination.

Dancing is erotic. His heavy breath. Sweat in the curls of his hair. His hips gyrating. I can easily imagine him in bed this way. Up against me. His lips against mine or pressing kisses down my neck. God, I can feel his hands. He's barely ever touched me and yet his touch burns against me in my imagination.

My hand moves quickly, no tenderness in my touch. And with each jerk of my fingers, my high increases. I lean up against the bathroom sink, gripping the edge until my knuckles are white as I push myself further and further.

I want him. I want him so bad. I want his green eyes to lock in mine as he thrusts in and out of me, I want his breath to stutter and his hips to jerk as he gets closer to coming inside me. I want his gruff, masculine voice to say my name with vulnerable want. "Rye... Rye... "

I teeter over the edge, my clit sending shocks of orgasm through me. I choke on a whimper, not wanting to draw attention to myself. Like a wilting flower, I droop forward, falling to my knees and resting my forehead on the cool ceramic of the sink. That'll cool me down, hopefully. Deep breaths, Rye. Deep breaths.

How am I going to face him now that I've touched

myself to the very thought of him? It's been hard enough to face him as it is.

Get a grip, Rye.

It's probably time to redownload Tinder. Get this energy out elsewhere.

I put myself back together, make sure that my face isn't too red or my pupils too dilated, wash my hands with at least three pumps of soap, and head back to the rehearsal hall.

The band has stopped playing and they're chatting back and forth with Ash affably.

"Sorry I had to step out," I announce.

Ash looks back at me, his green eyes boring into mine as if he knows that's not the whole truth.

"We thought you hated us!" DJ cries out and the whole band laughs.

I step over toward Ash, just far enough that I know I won't be able to smell his cologne. He gives me a sidelong glance. "What do you think?"

"I loved them," I say. "I really did."

"Me too. Do you think Clay and Giselle will think we're punishing them with a disco band?" Ash asks with a bold grin. I don't think he's been this relaxed around me since we started planning the wedding. I want to keep it that way.

"Maybe I should check in with them and then we can confirm with DeFUNK," I say and then turn to the band. "You were amazing. Can I be in touch later tonight to confirm?"

DJ puts on a playful thinking face. "You know, DeFUNK is in high demand, but I'll hold off your date until you get back to us tonight."

I laugh. Their energy is so good and all encompassing, I

almost forget I was just touching myself to the thought of Ash in the bathroom.

"I'm in as long as we can get a bit of Donna Summer on the setlist," Ash says. So, he's a closeted disco fan... who would've thought.

"Please, you don't think we've got Donna on the playlist? Man, you trippin'," DJ snorts. "We do the uncut version of 'Love to Love You Baby'. Moans and all!"

The blood rushes from my face. Moans and all.

"That's the way I like it!" Ash says back and the two of them laugh.

Fuck.

Chapter 8

Ash

I feel like I'm trapped in a small space, being squeezed into my seat by invisible walls. I stare at the table in front of me covered in a pristine white tablecloth. Across from me, Rye. Always Rye. I can't bear to look at her. Otherwise, I'll feel like we're on a date or something.

I hear the slight, tiny sound of metal scraping and let my gaze raise briefly. Rye is running the charm on her necklace back and forth, over and over. Her eyes dart around the shop nervously as if someone might jump out and scare her.

"Alright, a flight of tastings for the beautiful couple," the pastry chef named Rita, says with excitement in her thick Colombian accent.

My eyes meet Rye's for the briefest moment; her entire face is flushed. "Thank you," I say in a pitifully small voice.

Neither of us had the heart to correct her about our status as a couple when we arrived. Almost every consultation we've had through planning, someone inevitably implies we are together. Rye has been very good about trying to communicate beforehand that we're here on behalf of Clay and Giselle, so it's usually just something we can have a polite laugh about.

But since the moment we walked in, Rita has practically insisted that we are the happy couple. We couldn't get a word in edgewise and now we're too deep in the lie.

"These look beautiful," Rye says, her voice delicate and shy, evoking the girl she used to be. It used to be the thing that made me able to resist her, the memory of her teenage self. Now, it just makes me marvel more at the woman she's become.

Rye has infiltrated most of my waking thoughts. Last night, when I was visiting with my granddaughter, Piper had to thwap me on my leg in the middle of a game of Candyland when I zoned out, thinking about Rye.

"It's your *turn,* Papa!" she squealed.

I apologized profusely and gave her a peppering of messy kisses, but I still couldn't shake the feeling of Rye.

Rita gives us an endearing smile with her raspberry pink lips and then walks us through the cakes she's given us samples of on the plate. Classic checkerboard chocolate and vanilla, lemon raspberry, and tres leches inspired. They all look incredible.

"I will leave you two lovers alone. Take your time. Enjoy it. Experience the tastes... " Rita runs her tongue around the inside of her mouth. "Savor the experience. This is such a special time. Don't let the planning and the anxiety overcome your love. Your intimacy."

I stare at the cakes with wide, glazed over eyes until I'm not looking at anything at all. I'm stuck on the word lovers. Been years since I've had a lover. After Rose's death, I've barely touched another woman. It's way too easy for me to picture Rye in that position. In all sorts of positions.

Nope. No. Stop right there. She's off-limits. Always. No amount of time or distance will change that she is Clay's daughter. That is always a part of Rye. And because of that, I can never have any of her. I have three single sons who would be much more age appropriate. I could set them up. If she likes kids, Jarred would be perfect for her. They're the same age and... who am I kidding? It would be impossible to have her around and not feel anything. I'd just be torturing myself further.

Rita leaves us with a flourish of her hands, sweeping out of the room dramatically. Rye and I both stare at the cake. We have to share the slices. Lord help us.

"She's a trip," I say quietly.

Rye giggles. "It's clear she loves what she does."

I chew on the inside of my lip and then lean forward suddenly. "Hey."

Her eyes widen, deer in the headlights. I've scared her.

"I hope I'm not making you uncomfortable."

Her brow furrows. "What? No, I—"

"I should have said something. About... " I gesture between the two of us. "That we're not... " I give her a half-smile.

Rye shakes her head. "No, I should have said something, it was—"

"There wasn't a good moment."

"Exactly. She just assumed and then—"

"*Right.* Totally."

"You didn't make me feel uncomfortable," Rye says firmly.

I swallow. At least she can't tell all the absolutely inappropriate thoughts I've had about her. "Good. That's the last thing I'd want."

"I know, Ash."

Fuck, my name flows out of her mouth like a gentle, melodic breeze. "We should have some cake."

"Yes!" she says excitedly and holds up her fork. "Where do you want to start?"

"Let's go classic and then work our way up, hm?"

We both scoop a piece of the checkerboard cake onto our forks and take a bite. It's moist and subtle in flavor. Shockingly both the chocolate and vanilla come through.

"Mmm... " Rye hums. Her eyes meet mine and she smiles before covering her mouth while she chews demurely.

"It's good," I say, going in for another bite.

"Wow, another bite, hm?" she teases.

I shrug. "I mean, I'm not going to say no to cake when it's in front of me."

"That's a good attitude."

"I couldn't live without sugar. I know some people do, but I just... sounds miserable," I remark before popping another bite in my mouth.

Rye sighs and clutches her heart. "Thank god you're not one of those."

"Right? Although I have to spend a lot of time in the gym to make up for it."

Her eyes briefly flick down to my chest and my pulse jumps the slightest bit to know she's looking at me. Maybe wondering what I look like underneath my dress shirt. *Cool it, Ash.*

"I'm going to start on the lemon and raspberry... " she says and cuts off a piece.

I watch as she puts the fork into her mouth, how her lips curl around the metal before she slides it back out. "How... how is it?"

Rye's eyebrows jump. "Oh shit. That's really good. Have a bite."

"Yes, ma'am," I chuckle and take my own bite of the lemon raspberry. Citrusy sweet with a bite of berry. It zings on the tongue and sends sparks down my spine. "Oh, man. That's dangerous."

"It's basically fruit. No gym needed," she says with a cheeky smile.

"Exactly," I say back.

We both indulge quietly in the lemon raspberry, taking extra nibbles, making sure our forks don't clink and that we don't take from the same areas, avoidant of even the intimacy of our forks accidentally mingling.

"Are you having fun?" I ask and immediately regret it because I sound like a dad who doesn't know how to talk to his teenage daughter.

"Eating cake? Sure, of course."

"But I mean, in the bigger sense," I say, putting my fork down. "You know, wedding planning. Are you enjoying it?"

Rye considers briefly, her eyes lolling to the side, a piece of lemon raspberry cake perched on her fork. "I mean, it's a lot of work. But it's been fun to look at all the options and make decisions. Pick out color schemes and things," she says and then eats the bite of cake. When she swallows, she adds, "Plus, it's unlikely I'll be doing this anytime soon for myself. Maybe it's kind of like practice."

"Oh, come on," I say wryly. "Surely, there's got to be someone."

She snorts. "Um. No. No one."

I don't want to feel relieved, but I do. "I'm shocked."

Rye looks into her lap. "Well, I... I don't know. It's hard to meet people that I actually like. My friends say my standards are too high."

"There's no such thing. That's what I'd tell my daughter if I had one," I say. This is good. I'm putting myself in the category of "dad." That's a good way to distance myself.

Her smile twists to the side and she errantly runs her fork through some lemon frosting. "Well, when you've been alone a while, I think there is such a thing as too high of standards." Rye's blue eyes slowly meet mine; I can't help but feel there's something behind her gaze. There's a story here or...

There's no possible way she could want me. *Get the idea out of your head.*

"Anyway," she says, effectively clearing the smoke of the subject away from the table, "I'm glad not to have to do it all alone. I would have already pulled most of my hair out."

I smile with surprise. "I'm glad I've become a serviceable assistant after the way things started off."

"You've made up for it. Especially watching you dance to Parliament," Rye says, pretending to wince.

"Woah, woah, woah! I think I've got some moves."

"Yes. *Some*," she reiterates.

I laugh. "Okay, maybe I need a drink or two to loosen me up, but you'll see. At the wedding, I'll be king of the dance floor."

"Oh, I look forward to it," she says with a waggle of her eyebrows.

Are we flirting? This feels like flirting. A little bit.

"Okay, what do we think?" Rita bombastically enters with a clap of her hands.

"The first two have been delicious, but I'm afraid we haven't made it to the last one," I apologize.

Rita gasps with a smile. "No, no. allow me to join you." She pulls up a chair to the table and leans on her elbows, grinning at us. "Okay. Go ahead."

Rye laughs nervously. "Oh, you're going to watch?"

"Yes! Yes, of course. It is so romantic to watch a couple share a bite of their wedding cake. Picture it, eh?" Rita grabs both of our forks and holds them out to us.

Rye and I exchange a look. She smiles. *Better do what she says.* We both take our forks from Rita.

"Picture it. You have just had the most special moment of your lives together. You are married. You have danced, you have been showered in love by your friends and family, you've had a delicious dinner and, now. Cake."

Rye and I both scoop up a piece of the final cake and start to bring it to our mouths.

"Ay! No! What are you doing?!"

We stare at her. "Eating... the cake... ?" I say, but I don't think this answer will suffice.

"You have to feed *each other*, dios mio," Rita says as if we are the biggest idiots on the face of the planet.

Rye and I exchange a frantic look. "Oh no," Rye attempts to intercede. "We don't—I'm a little—I don't like to be fed, I—"

"You need to practice for your big day! Everyone will be expecting it."

I purse my lips and give Rye a sympathetic look. Rita isn't giving us much of a choice. I'm afraid if we deny her, she'll have a heart attack. "Come on, honey," I say, playing into the role just a bit. We can at least make it silly. "Just this once."

Rye looks taken aback. She pauses, recalibrates, and then nods. "Just this once, *darling*."

I have to contain my laughter. She's laying it on as thick as mortar on brick.

"Good girl," Rita says. "Okay. Now, the cake. Go."

I bring my fork toward Rye first, prompting her to

follow suit, and with mirroring motions, we bring the forks to each other's mouths. I can barely concentrate on opening mine, though. I am watching hers intently. Her tongue darts out slightly to catch the fork before guiding it into her mouth. This feels more intense than when I watched her mouth earlier. The fork feels like an extension of me. An extra digit.

My cock jumps. I tighten my thighs.

Rye bats her mascara laden lashes. It's not purposeful, but it may as well be from how it makes me feel. What am I going to do with her? We still have a little more than three months until the wedding and the planning is just going to get more and more intense.

"You have to open your mouth," Rita says, nudging me with her foot

"Right! Right," I say. What an idiot. I open my mouth and let Rye put the bite of cake into my mouth. She smiles sweetly at me, like *I'm* a child. That pretty little smile... pretty mouth...

I swallow, not even tasting the cake. "Mm. Good."

"Delicious. They've all been delicious."

I dissociate through the rest of the conversation with Rita. When Rye asks me which cake I like best, I default to her. I don't care. My mind is in two different, equally dark places. On one hand, I'm dealing with the guilt of yearning after my best friend's daughter. The same age as my son. Just an innocent young woman that doesn't deserve my perverse desire for her.

And on the other... there's Rose.

It's been more than ten years. Every day, I miss her and think about her. I wish she was here. I still love her so much. She was the love of my life. There's no point in pursuing anything with another woman, ever.

The few sexual encounters I've had since her death (of which I can count on one hand), I haven't enjoyed. There is an insurmountable guilt I feel, as if I've betrayed Rose's memory. The mother of my children. She gave me everything. And when we were only seventeen, I was a stupid boy who got her pregnant. She never hesitated.

Rose loved me unconditionally, with everything she had, until the day she died. I owe her... everything.

"You alright?" Rye asks.

I break out of the dark place briefly to respond. "Yes. Fine." I'm being cold again, but I can't help it. It's nothing to do with her. Or everything to do with her. I'm not sure. "If you don't mind, Rye, I'll leave you to tie up the loose ends. I've got some calls I have to make and... " My lips contort as if I've eaten something extremely bitter.

"Sure. No problem," she says, although I detect an edge of disappointment in her voice. I can't look at her face to confirm this.

"Let's touch base next weekend about next steps," I say, shoving myself away from the table and getting to my feet. I shake Rita's hand. I do not doubt she thinks I'm a horrible fiancé for treating this like a business transaction. Maybe Rye will explain the truth after I've left.

I leave the bakery and climb into my car. As soon as the door shuts, the darkness returns, emotion upheaving through my body. I bend over the steering wheel and cry. In mourning of Rose, in perverse broken hope for Rye, in guilt for my friendship with Clay.

I have to take these moments with myself. There's no way the world can know this part of me. The part that can so easily crumble.

I am weak. A slave to both my desire and to my grief. And the only way I can protect anyone, my friends, my family, and beautiful, sweet Rye, is to keep this misery all for me.

Chapter 9

Rye

Listen, I am a privileged person. I grew up not wanting for money in a stable home with my mom and my dad. I went to good schools and have a support system in everything I do.

However, the level of privilege Ashton Hawthorn knows is on a completely different level.

I've driven out to his home in the northern suburb of Wilmette. I feel bad now for all the times he's driven around to meet me based on his daily commute, but that disappears soon after I see the size of the homes in his neighborhood.

Mansions would be the correct way to describe them. Sprawling, grand structures that take up God knows how many square feet. I'm pretty sure none of his kids still live with him. What's a single billionaire doing in a stodgy mansion up in Wilmette?

Ash's house is right across from the Baha'i temple, one of the only ones in the world. I've been up here several times to walk the grounds and never even contemplated who or what was down the short dead ends right across the street. Turns out, it was Ash Hawthorn all along.

As I turn down the gravel driveway, I feel like I'm going to be persecuted for trespassing in my little Nissan. The L-shaped mansion is boastful and grandiose. To the right, three garage doors. I wonder how many cars he has squirreled away in there. To the left, I can see Lake Michigan through the trees that are now bountiful with leaves. Evening glow. June in Chicago can be chilly, but it's fucking beautiful. There are patches of flowers peppering the grounds that are lush and divine. It's hard for me not to get caught up in the flora and fauna anywhere I go.

I bring the car to a stop and before I even get out, Ash appears at the front door framed in ivy. Even at home, he's still dressed to the nines in navy slacks and a white dress shirt. The only thing different is his loafers, which he now wears stylishly without socks.

Ash gives me a wave with his big hand and I practically swoon at the size of it. He's got his phone pinned to his ear, trapped in the middle of a conversation.

Busy. Even on the weekend. Must be miserable. But when you have a house like this...

I get out of the car and immediately feel like I should have dressed nicer, even though I spent two hours slaving away over my appearance, trying to get that perfect I-don't-care-I'm-just-naturally-pretty look. I'm wearing tight jeans and a tight, lavender top, and some black heeled boots. Which seemed totally fine until my dad remarked on my way out the door, "Who are you all dolled up for?"

Talk about feeling guilty. The more I nurse this crush, the guiltier I feel. My poor dad just wanted someone to help me out. Not someone for me to thirst over. *His best friend.* That's a no-go. When I was a kid, it didn't matter. Now I'm an adult. And if I make stupid choices, people *will* hold me accountable.

Including Dad.

As I approach Ash on the front stoop, he finishes his up his call in clipped short words. "Yeah. Yeah, I hear you. I got to—I have to go. I'll send the paperwork over in ten. Yeah, yeah." He hangs up and tucks his phone into his pocket with a sigh. "Sorry about that."

"No worries. Thanks for having me. Your home is... " Eludes all adjectives. "Big."

Ash laughs. "Good observation."

We stand there for a moment. Feels like we should hug maybe or greet each other with more than just pleasantries. After all, we've spent quite a few days together over the past three months.

"Come on in," he says, pushing the door open for me and stepping aside.

"Thank you," I remark. The inside of Ash's home defies description as well. The entry hall is tiled black and white with a huge chandelier overhead and a staircase curling up to the left. "Wow," I say quietly.

Ash closes the door and walks in with purpose. "If you don't mind, I just have to get some paperwork settled and sent off and—"

"Of course. Take your time."

He folds his hands as if in prayer. "I'm so sorry about this, Rye. I thought I'd have everything finished but—"

"it's totally fine. I promise." The whole reason I came to meet *him* was that he'd been hit with a bombshell at work and had been doing damage control all day. It only makes sense he's still tying up loose ends.

Ash smiles. "Promise. Ten minutes and then I'm all yours."

All yours. I like the sound of that.

"Go ahead and make yourself at home. There's coffee

brewing if you want some. I thought we could set up in the dining room," he says, gesturing through the entry way before darting off toward his office.

The silence as soon as he's gone is overwhelming. I walk through the entryway and wince at the sound of my heels on the floor. The house opens up divinely, with big picture windows giving stunning views of Lake Michigan. The Eastern sky is warm with swathes of orange and pink. I stand, captivated for a few moments, before following the smell of coffee brewing in the kitchen.

Do I need to go into detail about the kitchen? It's beautiful just like everything else in this godforsaken house. It's state of the art, it's divine!

I pass through the kitchen into the dining room, which has a long, dark wooden table with a beautiful arrangement of lilies right in the center. I drop my bag on one of the chairs and begin to unpack. In classic event planner fashion, I have made a binder to keep track of everything. It has pockets and pull outs which I begin to disassemble and spread out purposefully across the table.

Ten minutes, though, turns into twenty. Turns into half an hour. Turns into... forty-five. I feel too uncomfortable to move from the dining room, even though I really have to pee. The sky outside is darkening. I try to find the light switch, but it must be hidden somewhere. Rich people. Nothing can ever look like the thing it is.

"What are you doing here in the dark?" Ash asks.

I jump at the sound of his voice. "You scared me!"

"Sorry! Sorry, I didn't mean to."

I turn to find him in the doorway of the dining room. "I can't find the light switch."

He frowns and looks askance to a white light switch

beside the door I completely missed. Fuck, he must think I'm an idiot. "Sorry, I got held up again with a call. It won't happen again." He flicks on the light and it immediately hurts my eyes. I didn't realize just how dark it had gotten. Ash scans the table. "Looks like you've already got everything ready to go."

"Yeah, I thought I'd get it all set up so we can just jump in."

Ash stares at me. Blinks. "Great."

"Great."

We stare at each other. Both of us quiet. Ash starts to walk into the room; I flinch reflexively. He stops and holds up his hands as if he's hurt me.

He scares me. Like I'm a deer and he's a wolf, except in this case, the thing at stake is not my life but... okay, never mind. It is my life. If I let him get too close, I might not be able to handle myself. I round the table to make sure I'm away from him.

"Where should we start?" Ash asks, hands in his pockets.

"I think décor details is going to be the most tedious thing," I say, opening up the binder to the décor tab. "They've sent over a lot of decisions we have to make about colors of linens and table arrangement."

Ash picks up one of the papers on the table and looks at it skeptically. "You mean, like seating arrangement?"

"No, no. Like how the tables are arranged. See, they gave us overhead visuals so we can decide if we want it in the round or like concentric circles or... " As I'm saying it, I realize how ridiculous it sounds. I hand Ash a stack of rendered images of tables and he takes them from me, his long fingers extending onto the page. He's got dark hair lightly trailing up the back of his hand. I hold my breath. He's all man.

As he thumbs through the pictures, he laughs. "Wow. This is intense, huh?"

"Weddings are no joke," I say with a tired smile.

"Right. Of course. I just... I'm a little out of my element," Ash says and then hands the stack back to me.

I frown. "What do you mean?"

"Well, the big things, I can discern what's good and what's bad, right? You know, lemon cake and disco bands."

"Sounds like a bad porno when you say it like that," I giggle.

For the briefest moment, his eyes glint, ready to pounce on the joke. He decides against it. "Yeah, well, these small things... I just really haven't conceptualized how much goes into all of it." I don't mean to urge him with my look, but my confusion is evident enough for him to clarify. "Rose... my wife... you know, she and I got married in her parents' backyard and Jarred—he was just a baby—he couldn't stop crying so she held him the whole ceremony."

I laugh, endeared to the memory. I had no idea that things with him and his wife had been unconventional that way. "That's really sweet."

"It worked out. Not all eighteen-year-olds who get married are ready for it, but it worked out for us," he says, his eyes landing on the table. "Mostly." Ash looks back at me and puts on a big, closed-lipped smile, cutting the memory of his wife's passing.

"We don't have to talk about it if you don't—"

"No, no, I don't mind at all. It's nice to remember her. I sometimes get too afraid to talk about her out loud like that will make it harder, but it always feels nice," he says. "It's like going to the gym."

I can't help but burst into laughter. "Grief gym."

"Exactly."

"I'm familiar."

The smile on his face fades. "Right. Yeah, of course." His eyes narrow. "Is this—is this hard?"

I frown in confusion. Being around him? Trying to not have a crush on him after thirteen years? "Sorry?"

"Your dad getting remarried."

"Oh." *I'm a dumbass.*

"I mean, you've always seemed to have a positive attitude about it. I just imagine that must be tough for you. After losing your mom."

I get the sense he's less asking so he can know how I'm doing, but to know how he can justify moving on. As far as I know, Ash hasn't had any relationships after his wife passed away. Over ten years. That's... a long time. "I love Giselle," I say with a smile of wonder. "I didn't think it was possible. When my dad told me met someone, I was scared that it would be some Cinderella story and I'd be stuck with an evil stepmother and stepsisters."

"Media isn't kind to the mixed family dynamic, isn't it?"

"At least not in Grimms' Fairytales."

Ash laughs. Every smile and laugh I get is like a little gift. I will cherish each one, especially since the first few times we saw one another, he was icy as the arctic. "Totally."

"Giselle, though, just fit right in. They got along so well and that made it easy to get along with her too. Neither of them forced me to like her, just let me come to it in my own time..." I pause and glance out the window. The lake is more obscured by darkness now. "I think it helped that she also knew loss. You know, they met in group therapy and—"

"Yes, I suggested he go."

"Really?"

"Yeah. I went there the first couple years after Rose died. Then I just... didn't have the time with Hawthorn expanding the way it did. Anyway. I interrupted you."

I shake my head. "It's okay. I didn't know you suggested he go."

Ash shrugs plainly. *No big deal.*

"Anyway, I eventually came around. And while I didn't have a new mom, I had a new person. That I just fucking adore," I say. "That I really am glad is in my life in such an important way. So... doing this for them is an amazing gift. A stressful gift, but an amazing one."

When I finally look at Ash, I see there are tears in his eyes. He tries to laugh at my last comment but is clearly wrapped up in his own thoughts. "Sorry, ehm." He clears his throat and flicks away the one tear that's freed itself from the corner of his eye. "I'm even more honored to be able to help you with planning this wedding."

I smile at him. "So. Table arrangements. Thoughts?"

We get through many of the decorating decisions at a breakneck pace. Ash and I work well together when we're focused. And, to my surprise, he's got quite discerning taste and opinions on almost everything. Our rapport is better than it's ever been, and even though I can't ignore I still want him, I at the very least can respect the relationship we do have. Dynamic wedding planning duo. Perhaps the next three months will go by quickly and smoothly now.

All of this comes to a halt when we try to decide napkin color. Fucking napkin color!

"Ecru."

"No, I hate it," I say, crossing my arms.

"It's classic. And it's classy."

"I much prefer the pearl."

Ash makes a gagging sound. "Are you kidding? It's totally tacky."

I crack a smile even though I'm willing to defend my choice to the death. "*Tacky*?"

"Yeah. I said it."

We stand on opposite sides of the table, his arms crossed, me with my hands on my hips. This feels... playful. Fun, even.

"I'm vetoing ecru," I say off-handedly.

"You already used your veto on the canopy lighting."

I roll my eyes. "Now, *that* was tacky."

"You're infuriating."

I bite my lip. I don't quite mind being infuriating, especially when he's looking at me with his head tilted to the side and his green eyes fixed in mine.

After a moment, Ash asks, "You hungry?"

I shake my head. Even though I could eat, I'm not feeling hungry. "No. I'm fine."

"You... want a drink?"

I smirk. "You're asking that as if it's illegal."

"I just don't want your dad to get mad at me for giving you alcohol," he says under his breath.

All the fun comes to an immediate halt with the mention of my dad. "I'm twenty-nine, Ash. I can drink without my dad's permission."

"Well, I know that, but... " Ash trails off and then nods. "Okay. Wine? Red or white."

"Red," I say.

"Coming right up."

When he returns with a bottle of wine and two glasses, he suggests we go sit outside for a bit since it's such a nice night. I agree and follow him outside, down a winding stone path to a rocky outcrop right at the edge of the property.

The water is just below, waves sloshing lightly against the retaining wall. Such a gorgeous sound.

"Do you sit out here a lot?" I ask, taking a sip of wine. Tangy and musky on my tongue. Would be easy to drink a whole bottle of this, I think.

"When I have the time. Which is rare. It's a good place to think," he remarks softly, looking into the bowl of his wine glass.

Liquid courage doesn't usually set in so fast, but my nerves have been so on edge all evening that it only takes a little wine to ply too many questions out of me. "You live here alone?"

"Yep."

"Sorry if that's an invasive question," I say. Big gulp of wine. Calm the nerves.

"No, no, you're right," he says. "It's weird, isn't it? To be in this big house all by myself. The boys all stayed with me until they were ready for their own space, you know? I mean Keifer only moved out... I guess it's over a year ago now. Huh. Time flies."

I look back at the mansion. So beautiful and big. "I bet it was a beautiful place for them to grow up in."

Ash smiles crookedly. "They only spent a bit of their childhood here. We really chose it for us. Me and Rose, I mean." He sighs. "We could picture the grandkids tumbling around the lawn and a big fucking Christmas tree in the living room and... " He laughs. "Life doesn't go to plan, does it?"

Even though he's talking about his wife who has passed, I'm even more infatuated. I've never seen this soft side. The few times I saw him when I was younger, he was ebullient, always quick with a joke or a laugh. The past three months have been completely counter to that in a lot of ways. Coldness, distance. And the undercurrent of it all is... this overwhelming love for his family. For his dead wife.

I want him even more.

"There are just too many memories here to leave it behind. You understand."

"Of course. My dad is the same way."

He nods solemnly.

I finish up my wine. Probably too quickly. If Ash thinks I'm a drunk, so be it. "I'm sure many women would be thrilled to live in a house like this."

Ash quirks his eyebrows as if I'm speaking gibberish.

"I just mean, if you didn't want to be alone, I don't think it'd be hard for you to fix that." *Wow, Rye.* Not only am I being super invasive, I'm speaking as if I've never crafted a sentence in my life.

"Oh, I don't know about that, Rye."

"I'm serious!" Doubling down. Might as well get some more wine. I fill both of our glasses, even though his is not yet drained.

Ash laughs uneasily. The thought of getting his best friend's daughter drunk before she has to drive back home into the city is probably weighing on his mind. "I'm kinda old. I'm a grandfather now."

I snort. "Oh, please. You wouldn't be able to tell. You're in good shape and—" I stop myself because if I start on the list of words to describe Ash, I'll make more a fool of myself than I already have. Ruggedly sexy... insanely attractive... utterly irresistible.

"Rye, you're very sweet, but—"

"No, no I'm not sweet," I say abruptly.

We stare at each other through the dark, only lit by some of the landscape lighting underneath bushes and trees.

"I'm telling you the truth."

Ash blinks. His silence kills me each second that passes. I'm waiting for him to tell me that it's time for me to go and then tomorrow morning find out he called my dad and said I was super disrespectful and he never wants to see me ever again (and yes, this may be for the best, but it would kill me before it did anything good).

Instead, he drains his glass of wine in one go and then shakes his head as if he was about to say something and decided against it. How I would kill to know what thought crossed his mind. "I don't want to be alone, but I don't feel like I have a choice really."

"Of course, you do," I say with a smile. "I mean, take a look at my dad."

"It's different. I know it doesn't seem like it from an outside perspective but—"

"I lost my mom too. I'm not an outside perspective."

Ash's eyes singe shut. "Right. I'm sorry. That's not what I meant." He takes a deep breath. "You and your dad had time to prepare. I didn't. Rose was in an accident. I wasn't ready for life to change like that. I don't mean that losing Heather, losing your mom, was any less painful. I just wasn't ready. I'm still not ready and it's been fifteen years."

I can't help myself. I reach out and grab his hand. I know he feels that we're different, but we're not. We're just not. I can feel him try to jerk away from me at first before settling into my touch.

His hand is warm and soft. Tucking my fingers into his palm makes them nearly disappear. It feels so nice. Not in that electric way I expected, but like lowering yourself into a warm bath. With bubbles and nice candles. Therapeutic in a way. "It's really hard," I say gently.

"It is." Ash's hand tightens on mine. I swear I feel him

tug on my hand slightly. Does he want me closer? It's all I've ever wanted.

But no. No, I can't. Not with my dad's best friend. I withdraw suddenly and get to my feet. "Okay, back to work," I announce and make my way back to the dining room, warm-faced and wobbly.

Ash calls out my name and follows me. I can't bear to look back. If the tug on my arm was my imagination, I need to get out of here. If it wasn't... I still need to get out of here.

I shuffle through papers as if it's purposeful. Ash appears in the door, but I don't look at him. "I don't know, I'm still not settled on how the tables should be set up."

"Then let's take a look," he says, his voice low and calm.

But instead of going to the opposite side of the table like we had been working the hour before, he comes up behind me, looking over my shoulder at the documents. I lean forward and slide the table arrangement blueprints back toward us. I point at something, anything. "This might be more conducive to foot traffic."

"Mm... I see what you mean," Ash replies. He puts his hand on the table by my hip and leans over my shoulder to look.

I can feel my heartbeat in my mouth. His closeness can't be an accident, can it? "What do you think?" I ask and turn my face toward him.

Ash looks back at me with hard intensity in his green eyes. His tongue quickly wets his lips. "I think I'm not thinking about table arrangements right now."

I stare back at him, terror and arousals mixing in my pelvis.

Ash apprehensively pushes a lock of my hair back from my face, tucking it behind my ear and I swoon at his touch, my eyes shutting and a sigh slipping from between my lips.

This feels like a dream, one I've had a million times and played out every aspect in such a way that it never could have happened.

Until now.

Ash cups the side of my face in his broad hand and then brings his lips to meet mine. I'm kissing Ashton Hawthorn. In fact, *he* kissed *me*.

He wants me. After all this time I've yearned for him.

I put my hand up against his chest and I can feel his heart thumping faster than the average beat.

Ash pulls away too soon for my liking and so I follow after his lips for more, pushing myself onto the tips of my toes and wrapping my arms around his neck to kiss him as deeply as possible. He grunts into my lips and wraps his arms around me.

There is no hesitation in our closeness. Chest to chest, hips to hips. I can feel all of him. His hardness.

He wants me. And I'll let him have me. If only once. I can deal with the guilt of just once.

For now, I cast any trepidation far away.

"Rye," Ash growls against me. "I want you so bad."

I run my hands through the wavy locks of dark hair. "Have me. Have me now."

Ash takes this as literally as he can. He pins me up against the lip of the table by his hips and in a fluid motion I've only ever seen in movies, swipes everything off the dining room table. Papers fly, the vase and lilies crash to the ground, I gasp. Ash kisses me and guides me back onto the table, in total control. Just the way I've always imagined he would be.

He drags his kisses down to my neck, his scruff scraping up against my skin. I moan. He could keep doing just that and I'd probably come.

For all the gentleness we gave one another outside, there is none here. As he works my neck, he aggressively undoes my jeans and pulls them down, leaving my panties exposed, a black mesh thong with a little bow. He lifts his head and smooths his thumbs over my hip bones. He swallows thickly, Adam's apple bobbing. "I want to taste you."

I'm at a loss for words.

Ash hooks his arms under my knees and lifts so my lower back is raised off the table. I let out a laugh of nervousness. He leans into my crotch and pushes his face into my panties, inhaling deeply. "Oh, fuck," he says, eyes rolling back. "You're not supposed to smell this good."

"I'm sorry," I say with a half-smile.

His eyes sharply catch mine. "No, you're not."

I can't help a mischievous giggle.

With unbearable slowness, Ash bites the waistband of my underwear and pulls them down so my pussy is exposed to him. My breath seizes.

His eyes don't leave mine as his tongue slinks out of his mouth and laps at my clitoris. My hips jerk, an electric pulse snapping through my body. I roll my head back with a sigh of pleasure.

Ash's lips and tongue work me with ease. When he groans into me, my bones shake. I've been waiting for this moment so long that I feel like I might come at any moment. I grab at his hair, pushing his face harder into my groin and he laughs against me.

My legs are shaking now. I've never had someone eat me out this voraciously and masterfully.

He pauses and licks his lips. "Taste so good. So wet."

I am rendered speechless with arousal blooming up my body. I reach for the collar of his shirt and pull him down to me.

Ash chuckles. "You want a taste, baby?"

I nod heavily. "Yeah, yes."

His lips crash onto mine and I embrace him as tight as possible to me. Ash's hands slide underneath my shirt, slipping around my breasts. "Fuck. *Fuck*. Your body is fucking perfect."

"Fuck me," I say suddenly. It just comes out. But it's all I want. I can't wait a moment longer.

Ash puts his thumb on my lower lip, holding my chin in his hand. "Say you want me inside you."

"I want you inside me so bad."

His eyelids lower. "Say you need me inside you."

I push my hips up toward his and he shudders. "Need you inside me. Now"

"You're so fucking good. You're so... " Ash kisses my jaw and my throat with hunger.

I reach down and undo the belt on his pants, sliding it off in a fell swoop. Apparently, I have some moves too.

In no time at all, he's released himself from his pants, his long, thick cock standing at attention. Ash jerks himself slowly and leans down to my ear. "Your pretty pussy needs my cock?"

Before I can respond, I feel the head of him sliding between my lower lips, teasing my opening. I gasp. "Yes, Ash."

The tip of his cock dips inside me shallowly and pops back out. I whine in disappointment and he chuckles. "I like the sounds you make, Rye." He nibbles my ear gently. "You know how bad I've wanted you?"

Wanted. Past tense. For how long, I don't know. But long enough to get here.

"Have I been obvious?" he questions further. The head

of him slides into my opening again, deeper this time. He does not retreat.

I shake my head. "No, I didn't... " I pause as a wave of pleasure hits me from how he's stimulating me from inside. "I didn't know."

"Didn't want you to," he breathes and slides deeper inside me. "Nngh... so tight."

I buck my hips toward him and Ash whimpers.

"So tight," he repeats, thrusting into me. Slow at first. Exploring my depths and tightness. With each pulse, I feel closer to euphoria. Inching at first and then, as he quickens, leaping toward it. Ash pushes one of my thighs back, widening me. he straightens up and then slams his whole length into me.

I squeal, back arching, head thrown back. I catch sight of the broken vase on the ground. I made him do that. I made him destroy things for me.

I'm a fucking goddess.

"You're so beautiful," he says breathlessly. "Look at you. Holy shit... " And this pushes him right over the edge, thrusting into me at a breakneck pace. His brow is furrowed in concentration, lips tucked back, grunting over and over.

"I'm going to come, I'm going to come, I'm going to—" I can't finish my thought before an aggressive, white heat shoots through my body. I screech in release, in pleasure, holding onto the lip of the table over my head to try and keep a grip on reality.

Ash lets out a stuttering yell that alternates between boisterous and completely silent as he lets go completely inside me. His warmth elongates my orgasm, all of my nerves smoldering.

As I try to catch my breath, I'm taken off-guard by Ash

wrapping his arms around me and lifting me into the air. I let out a laugh of surprise. "Where are you taking me?"

"Bed," Ash replies and kisses me harshly. "Now."

I gasp. "More?"

A hungry smile appears on his ruby lips. "Much more."

Chapter 10

Ash

I tap my thumb against the counter, watching the coffee drip into the pot. I've never understood the need for over-fancified espresso machines when a cup of drip coffee gets the job done the same way.

It's later than I usually wake up. I'm normally pretty militant about my alarm, but after last night, I needed an extra hour to sleep.

Rye and I went at it all night. I didn't know I had that kind of stamina to come and come and come, but... she just brings that energy out of me. Just as I predicted, Rye is all woman. It was easy to forget about the danger of getting close to her.

Some of the night is hazy. I can't really pinpoint the moment my defenses broke down, especially when combined with the wine. I wasn't drunk, I don't think, but the adrenaline combined with the alcohol does dangerous, wild things to a person.

I knew once I got out of bed, we'd have to forget about it. So, I relished the morning too.

Waking up next to Rye was a dream I didn't know I

had. For the first time in years, I wasn't alone. I could turn over and find someone in bed next to me. Her body fit perfectly in the spot next to mine. I couldn't resist curling around her and holding her.

It was all better than I possibly could have imagined.

And now I hate myself.

I did the thing I knew I couldn't. The thing I knew I'd regret.

If the night could exist in a vacuum, then of course, I wouldn't regret sleeping with Rye. But it doesn't. So I do.

I regret it.

"Good morning."

I turn to find Rye in the doorway of the kitchen. Her dark hair is frizzed and musted and her eyes are dark like a racoons having not removed her makeup from the night before. She's wearing my black robe with the red stripes. It goes all the way to her calves, making her look tiny. Like a child. I can't get that image out of my head. She's just a kid. Maybe not literally. And while I'm old enough to be her father, it's not as dramatic as a gap could be. But shouldn't your friend's children be like your own?

Yes. I'm going to say yes. You should not sleep with your friend's children.

"I hope it's okay I put on your robe, I didn't have anything else and I—"

"It's totally fine. Hi. Good morning." I'm all backward. All turned around. "Coffee?"

She smiles shyly. "Sure. Thank you."

I pour two mugs of coffee. It's all I can focus on. Coffee. The color of coffee, like that of Rye's hair. The smell of coffee, intoxicating like the scent of her sweat. The taste of coffee, delicious like her.

I know how she tastes. I know how she feels. I know too much.

I hand her one of the mugs. Her hands wrap around the cup so delicately. God, I'm so fucking whipped that even the way she holds a mug of coffee gets me hard.

I clear my throat. "Did you sleep okay?"

Rye nods through a sip of coffee.

"Good, good."

"Did you?"

"Fine."

"Good."

This is painful. I have to get her out of here. But I can't be cruel.

Rye chews on her lower lip and takes a seat at one of the bar stools at the end of the island. "You won't tell my dad, will you?"

I guffaw despite myself. "Uh, no I won't."

"Good," she says, scooching her mug back and forth over the counter gently.

"You... you won't tell him either, right?"

"God no," she says with a solemn smile.

I nod. "Good. Good."

Without having to initiate a let's-talk-about-what-happened conversation, it's been set in motion naturally. Just as things went last night. It felt natural. That's what's so painful about all of it. It felt natural, but it's so incredibly unnatural.

"It was... fun," I say, trying to remain didactic.

"Yes, I agree."

I have to keep my heart from fluttering at the news that she also had a good time. I've been so out of practice with the whole sex thing I was worried I might be amateurish. "And we should probably just... you know."

"Pretend like it didn't happen," Rye replies matter-of-factly.

I'm surprised she's the one to say it, and though I should be grateful, I feel a little scathed. That doesn't make sense, though. Wouldn't it just make it worse if she decided she wanted it to happen again? "Yes. Exactly."

Rye nods and looks into the pool of brown liquid in her mug. "We've got most everything under control for the wedding for the next month or so. So maybe we can limit seeing each other until we absolutely have to."

No Rye. This is for the best. But I already feel my heart yearning to be near her.

"Because that was really great and I'd hate to... I don't know, make a mistake or not be able to handle myself or be weird or awkward around you. Maybe we can just reset and pretend like it didn't happen," she says, her lips smiling but her eyes glassy and distant.

Have I hurt her? Did I force her to do something she didn't want? "I'm sorry, Rye, I shouldn't have—"

"Don't apologize," she says adamantly. "Really, I... I wanted to."

Me too. I don't say it out loud.

"My dad can just never know. Ever."

"Of course."

Her brow scrunches in the middle as if she's about to cry. How could I be so selfish to put her in this position?

"Rye—"

"I'm going to get out of your hair," she says with a smile, getting off the stool and ambling toward the kitchen door again.

I nod. "I wish I had some clothes to offer you, or—"

"That's alright."

"You could take a shower, if you wanted."

She shakes her head vehemently. "No, no, I'm just going to get dressed and go."

We stare at each other. So much to be said and yet... nothing. Nothing at all.

I still feel the undercurrent of desire for her. My gut is urging me to go toward her. Kiss her once more. But once would turn into twice would turn into never letting her go. And I have to let her go.

Rye goes to change. She's so quiet that she slips out the front door without me realizing and by the time I do, she's already peeling out of the driveway.

Distance is the only thing that will fix this. Distance, time, and moving on. This is why I was so cold to her when we first met up. I knew that with even an inch of kindness, I would lose my ground. Look where my lack of self-control has gotten us.

When I check my phone, there's a text from Clay.

Rye didn't come home last night. Did she stay with you?

I want to vomit. It's like he knows. A father's intuition is intense. I should know. But I imagine it's even stronger when you have a little girl.

Yep. She just left. Ended up working really late last night, didn't want her driving so far in the dark.

A moment. And then—

Thank you :)

I've never wanted to die more than right now.

* * *

Family dinners can sometimes be poorly timed, but none more than this one. Just yesterday, Rye woke up in my bed. The house has not yet shed her energy and I'm worried everyone can feel it. That's why I've decided to have dinner out on the terrace. After all, it's a gorgeous Chicago evening and as the nights get longer and the weather warms up, there's no reason *not* to be outside.

At least that's my excuse.

"How's the wedding planning going, Ash?" June asks mid-dinner. We are enjoying our fresh grilled fish—courtesy of grill-master extraordinaire, Oliver—with zucchini spears and a summery pasta salad. At least for the grown-ups. Piper's opted for a simple plate of pasta and some broccoli which Jarred is currently negotiating with her to eat.

I clear my throat. June's asked every time I've seen her. She really *is* into weddings I guess. "It's good," is all I can manage, even though I'm sure that's going to draw suspicion.

June looks to Keifer so fast I almost don't catch it. They know each other so well that they have an unspoken language. Even though it's momentary, they've just had a whole conversation with one look. She's probably worried she's asked something she shouldn't since I didn't say more.

"I mean..." I can't leave June hanging like that. "It's kind of like a second job. Forgive me if I'm not thrilled to talk about it."

She smiles, face filled with understanding, "I get it. Don't worry about it."

I smile back and then start to chew on my lower lip like it's a piece of gum. My pulse has not settled since Rowan and Trevor arrived, early might I add, and Rowan held up a bottle of tequila and excitedly announced her promotion as a systems administrator at the tech company she works for. I've had to refuse about three times. At my age, I can't drink tequila unless I've cleared my schedule for the week.

I'm worried they can smell her on me or see the traces of her in the air. I vacuumed every inch of the rooms we were in case there were strands of her hair. I'll admit, I'm a bit paranoid.

But with guilt like this, how could I not be?

The conversation moves on. Keifer and June start talking about a concert they went to earlier in the week. Haim, or something.

"Listen, I'm not a fan. I just go with her because we're concert buddies, you know?" Keifer says defensively.

"Oh, stop *lying*, Keifer. Your nose is growing."

Piper giggles and points at her uncle. "You look like Pinocchio!"

June grins at the little girl. "I can always count on Piper to be on my side." June's a nanny herself and has a perfect rapport with Pipes. I know we're all grateful for the kind-hearted energy she brings to the table. "He knew all the words to all the big hits and –"

"Okay! I know a couple top forty songs! Sue me!"

"And when one of them started telling this story about her boyfriend, he *actually cried.*"

Keifer rolls his eyes. "You cried too!"

"It was a sad story, of course I cried!"

"That doesn't mean I'm a fan! You enjoyed Dead and Company last summer, but you hate John Mayer."

June twists her lips in thought. "That's true. I don't like John Mayer."

"My point."

Rowan grabs the tequila bottle in the middle of the table and holds it up. "Who is doing another shot with me?"

"Ro, we've all got work in the morning. It's your first day of your promotion!" Trevor says, pulling back on her arm.

"Unlike you, Trev, I can hold my tequila. June?"

June considers, but the smile on her face says it all. "Yes. I'm doing it."

"Count me in," Oliver adds.

"Me too!" Piper cries out.

We all laugh. "You can have your own shot of water, Pipes," Oliver says, leaning over into his niece's seat and smooching her.

"I think we'll leave the shots out of it. I don't want her to be glorifying that just yet," Jarred says uneasily, eyeing me for some back up.

"Oh, crap, we're out of limes," Rowan says. "Let me go cut some up."

"Rowan, your language," Trevor reminds her.

"Sorry. Oh, crud. Better?" she asks dryly and then kisses Trevor's head before going inside to cut up more limes.

"Come here, Piper. I'm not doing a shot either. You can sit with the cool kids," I say, inviting her into my lap.

Piper leaps down from her chair and scrambles over to me whilst Rowan tries to convince everyone else to have a shot. She climbs up into my lap and starts to chew on the skirt of her dress. "Are you eating your dress?" I ask incredulously.

She pulls it out of her mouth. This is a habit we've been trying to break her out of for a couple months now. "No..."

"Because dresses, Piper, are not for eating. They're for *wearing*," I explain.

Piper laughs and then puts her dress back in her mouth.

"No, no, no! Not eating! Wearing!"

She laughs harder. We have this back and forth for a bit. She's my greatest distraction. Whenever I'm with

Piper, the rest of my mind is cleared out. There's only her. That's something I find so remarkable about children. They are extremely complicated and require so much work, but they are also so captivating. Every part of me, since Piper has been born, has been beholden to her. It was that way with my boys too. All I want is for her world to be wonderful.

"Well, well, well," Rowan's voice commands all of our attention as she exits the house.

I turn to look at her and immediately feel the color drain from my face. In one hand, she has a bowl of limes. In the other, Rye's binder.

Rye's fucking binder.

Where the fuck did she find that?

"What's that?" June asks.

Rowan props the binder up in the crook of her arm. "Clay and Giselle's Wedding Plans. This yours, Mr. H?"

I open my mouth, but all that comes out is a wordless sound.

"Oh, I want to see! Can we see, Ash?" June cries out, leaping out of her chair.

I grab tight to the arms of my chair. I have to stay composed. "Go ahead, take a look. Just... be careful."

Rowan and June hurriedly clear off a spot on the table and open up Rye's wedding binder. They're not the only ones intrigued; of course, Piper wants a look. She rushes over to June and June picks her up without hesitation. And Keifer and Oliver want in on the action, even if they're trying to act like they aren't interested.

"Oh, look at the ballroom. That's so pretty," June remarks.

"And the flowers. I love these colors," Rowan adds.

They gush for a couple more seconds, before Keifer

points to a page and frowns. "That's not your handwriting, Dad."

I clasp my hands over my stomach. My insides are churning. "No, sorry. No. That's Rye's binder."

"What are you doing with Rye's binder?" Oliver frowns.

One of those moments. Where I suddenly have everyone's attention. If I tell the truth, I'm scared they'll see it on my face, that Rye was at the house... and it wasn't just as innocent as wedding planning. But if I lie, I feel like they'll see right through that too. "She gave it to me so I could tinker with the seating arrangements. You know those things are like a puzzle. Who doesn't want to sit next to whom, where to put all the leftovers. It's a nightmare," I say casually.

The silence that follows is the longest of my life, even though it can't be more than a second.

"Oh my god, are those the bridesmaid's dresses? I'm obsessed," Rowan says, effectively moving past the conversation.

"Oooh. Pretty..." Piper agrees.

The excitement over Clay's wedding plans continues and I fade into the background. I get Jarred and Trevor to help me clear the dishes while everyone else enthuses.

The rest of the evening goes off without a hitch. No one suspects that something happened between me and Rye, let alone that she's been at the house at all. It might be all those tequila shots. Or maybe my guilt is a lot bigger than the situation actually is.

But that's the thing about guilt. It's like fire. If you keep feeding it, it only grows. If you don't put it out, it'll burn you alive.

And I can't afford to be burned alive. Even by Rye.

Chapter 11

Rye

I would like to say that in the month since I've seen Ash, I've been able to forget about him. But that would be an abject lie.

He's visited my dreams almost every night, recreating pieces of the night we spent together, making me have to remember each and every day what happened between us.

I'm able to distract myself for the most part during the day. Despite most of the planning having happened for the wedding, there are still plenty of duties to attend to. Most recently, Giselle and I went dress shopping. This is proving difficult as we're only two months away from the wedding so we either have to find a gown that fits off the rack or go in a more nontraditional route.

"Well, what do you think of this one?" Giselle says, coming out of the walk-in closet in another white gown ordered from Etsy.

We have not had "the" moment yet. The one where we look at each other and know it's the one. And this dress falls short of this expectation too. "It's not making me cry," I say sadly.

"Look, we're going to have to settle for something," Giselle says with a huff, running her hands down the waist of the dress.

"I mean, you look beautiful. Don't get me wrong. It's just... "

Giselle rolls her eyes.

"What?! Do you love it?"

"No! I just wanted you to love it and then maybe I'd love it," she says.

I laugh. "Well, you're the one who needs to love it, Elle."

She grunts and walks over to the full-length mirror in the corner of the room she shares with my dad. "I don't need to love it. I just need to be able to wear something. A sheet will do just fine at this point."

"Try it on, maybe it'll make me cry."

Giselle laughs despite her frustration and shakes her head at me. "Oh, Rye. You're a pain in the neck."

I grin. "Anymore?"

"One. But it's a little different."

"I like different. Let's see the different one."

Giselle shuffles out of the room and back into the closet. Even though Giselle is more like a friend than a new mother, our dynamic feels that intimate. She has no children of her own and has been told by doctors that it'd be nearly impossible for her to conceive. She sometimes jokes that she got all the benefits of a little girl without all the lost sleep, but deep down I know that she wishes she could have that.

I hope she can too. Even if it'd be weird to have a baby sibling at twenty-nine years old.

"Okay... " I hear Giselle sigh from the other room.

"Everything okay?"

"Um, yeah. Yeah." She comes out of the closet in an orange lace dress with gorgeous puffed sleeves. The color contrasts gorgeously against her dark skin. Giselle smiles at me sheepishly. "What do you think?"

Even though it's not even zipped up and I can't see how it hugs her figure, I feel tears come into my eyes. "Oh my god."

"You're crying!" she shouts excitedly. "I made you cry!"

"It's beautiful. It's perfect," I blubber. I help her zip it up and admire her in the mirror before us. "Elle, what the hell? You didn't tell me you were a supermodel?"

"Oh, Rye, hush."

I preen the dress gently, straightening out wrinkles, fluffing the shirt. "I'm serious. This is just incredible."

"I didn't think I wanted anything necessarily unique in the wedding," she says with a sigh, obviously starry-eyed at the dress. "You know, but I saw this one and I thought... you know. Weddings are such joyful events, I thought why don't I bring the color?"

"You bring the color wherever you go, Elle!"

Giselle gags. "You cornball!"

And I laugh. "I'll be your cornball every day."

"The rest of my life, hopefully," she says with a proud smile.

I stand outside the venue in Logan with two coffees. A peace offering maybe. I remember Ash's order. We've shared enough coffees over our months of working together that I know how he takes it. Hot black coffee, one sugar. Even in the summer. Which I think is insane. But then again, I drink iced coffee year round. This is my third of the day because I'm so nervous.

I haven't seen Ash since we... yeah. I don't know how to describe it. I could be didactic and say, "The night we had sex," or I could be crude and say, "The night we fucked," or I could be the hopeless romantic I've been since the very day I was born and say, "The best fucking night of my life."

I don't even think I'm overexaggerating. The things we did, the way we did them... it was absolute heaven. All of the things I hadn't felt before with men, I felt with him. Maybe because he's older and has more experience, he knows how to please a woman.

Not to mention, I had dreamed about that night since I was sixteen years old. I have never been able to get him out of my mind. Never thought it possible he would want me like I want him.

But at least for one night, he had.

Since then, our communication has been... distant. Emails mostly. Always from his work email, so there's no personality, no friendliness. Most always I'm just sending him details from vendors, hiccups in the budget, questions about meetings.

Now, though, with the wedding just two months out, we're going to have to get back on the grind. Which starts today with a visit to the venue. I offered to go by myself, but Ash said it'd be fine.

Well, really, he wrote over email, *I'll be there.* Just like that.

My phone starts buzzing in my purse. Shit, what if it's him? What if he's running late or something? I tenuously balance the cup of coffee on the other and pull out my phone. *Dara.* Shit. She's been calling me a lot lately and I just haven't been picking up. I'm not avoiding her per se. Just... I'm busy. And there's a lot on my mind.

And I can't afford to have someone gassing me up about having sex with Ash. Because there's no way that I can keep a secret from Dara. But a quick chat while I'm waiting won't hurt.

"Hello?"

"There she is! I thought the windy city might have blown you away!" Dara replies, laughing at her own joke.

"Hardee har har."

"Seriously, Rye? Where the hell have you been?"

I sigh. "Sorry, Dar. It's been crazy planning this wedding."

"I'm sure, but I was hoping for some more deets on the Ash-yay Awthorn-hay ituation-say..."

"Why are you talking in pig Latin?"

Dara laughs again. "I don't know! Seems like a situation that requires discretion."

"And what could be more discreet than pig Latin... Right."

Dara tsks. "I'm serious, Rye! Is everything okay?"

I swallow. How can I answer her and not lie? That's the name of the game. "Yeah. It's okay."

"So? Have things gotten better or...? Last I heard you were going cake testing something."

I smile. That was a nice day. That was before things got complicated. "Um. Things have been fine. Not a lot of planning. Just the little details."

"So, there's seriously no juice?"

I pucker my lips. It's a good thing she's not here right now because she would be able to tell I'm lying without blinking an eye. "No juice. Just wedding planning."

Ash's sports car pulls into a spot down the street and I

immediately feel my stomach flip flop. I could puke right now. I want to run, but my feet are glued to the ground. I have to face this. I'm going to have to face it at the wedding. In fact, I'll have to walk down the aisle on his arm, share a dance with him, pretend like things are fine.

Maybe we can even *make* things fine by then.

"Hey, Dar! I have to go. We're about to – I'm meeting Ash and –"

"Okay, call me right after. I want the details!"

"I know. I mean, I will. Love you, bye." I hang up and drop my phone back in my purse.

Before I even see Ash get out of the car, I see someone else get out of the passenger seat, someone even taller than him, his face echoed with features of Ash. This must be one of his sons. I'm not sure which. They all are like the spitting image of Ash from the few times I've met them. His son wears a casual blue suit with a tropical shirt underneath as if this is the Cayman Islands and not Chicago.

I only brought one other coffee. I don't have anything to offer. That's going to look suspicious. Needy. Like I'm not over it. And I need Ash to believe I'm over it. That we're good.

There's no trash can nearby and, while I'm a lover of all things nature (I'm a florist after all) I chuck the hot coffee over my shoulder into a bush as quick as possible, like it's a nervous tick, and then plaster an agitated smile on my face.

"Are you Rye?" Ash's son says as he approaches me, leaning to the side to examine me better.

"Yeah. That's me."

"Holy shit, I didn't recognize you at all. You look great," he says and comes over to me with his arms open for a hug. "How are you?"

He squeezes me so tight I can feel his muscles bulging. "Good!" I squeak.

As soon as the man releases me, I notice Ash over his shoulder, a bit at a distance. He's gotten a haircut since I last saw him, the sides cropped tighter to his head, and his stubble is well shaped. "Rye, good to see you."

"You too," I say in a voice lighter than air. I'm retreating to that shy girl I was when I was a kid. Fuck.

In his hand, he holds my wedding binder. I haven't seen it in a month and been totally lost without it. I bet he's organized it completely wrong. "You left this in my car last time," he says coolly and hands it to me.

I take it without thanks.

"I hope you don't mind I brought Oliver with me."

I expect him to have some excuse for why he brought Oliver (*yes, Oliver*). I wonder how he convinced him his presence was needed here today. "Of course! The more the merrier."

"Thought you two could catch up," Ash says over his shoulder as he goes toward the entrance. "Shall we?"

Oliver extends his arm. "After you."

"Thank you," I say softly. Oliver touches me politely on the back as I pass him. Fuck. Is this a setup? Is Ash trying to divert my attention with his spawn? That's... low. I mean, Oliver is obviously attractive. He's a bit rougher than I usual go for, with tattoos on his knuckles and bulging muscles everywhere you look.

I follow Ash inside. It's impossible not to look at his ass in his linen suit. I want to take a bite out of it. I get flashbacks of our night together, of gripping his naked ass hard as he fucked me for the third time, wanting to make impressions in his skin that would last forever.

"Rye, Ash! Good to see you!"

I snap out of my daydream as Dani comes toward us beaming. We hug politely. Ash introduces Oliver to her. "Just an extra set of eyes."

Does he not trust my eyes anymore? I have half a mind to make them both leave.

We ride up in the tight little elevator and now, instead of being dwarfed by one giant, I'm dwarfed by two. This is the makings for a really ridiculous amateur porno. I feel hot around the collar, but not in a fun way. In an absolutely mortified way.

I can smell Ash. And now that I've had him, every part of me needs him. Needs to touch, needs to taste. I only had him in my mouth such a short time. I wish I could have him again.

Okay, this is not going well.

We re-tour the venue, Dani talking about all our various specs and the decorations we've chosen. We work out some details about the band placement given that it's a larger ensemble than the venue is used to. The entire time, Ash moves in such a way that he keeps Oliver between me and him at all times. This is for the best. But he's sending a definite message. *There will be no more mistakes.*

Was it a mistake? Yes. Do I regret it?

I don't know that yet.

Oliver is affable and sweet, but I don't get the vibe he's into me or at least doesn't know how to flirt well. That's just fine with me.

"Now, the canopy lighting—" Dani begins.

I immediately interrupt. "No, that's not what we specified."

She frowns and looks through her iPad at all her various notes. "I'm sorry, that's what I have down."

I glare at Ash. Is he doing this on purpose?

"I may have... we had an incident with all the planning documents, I might have accidentally gotten some things turned around," he says carefully.

Incident is an understatement. "There will be no canopy lighting. We wanted the modern package with the string lights. And while we're at it, you don't have that the napkin color should be ecru, do you?"

Dani smiles and shakes her head. "Ivory."

I breathe a sigh of relief.

"My mistake," Ash says in a firm, gruff voice.

"Yes," I reply in such a way that someone might not be sure if I'm being unkind or I just don't know how to talk to people.

His eyes flash for a moment and then he shakes it off.

The rest of the tour we keep quiet. Nothing else inflammatory comes up.

Our goodbyes are cordial. Oliver gives me a hug again before I go off to my car.

It could have gone worse, I suppose. But there was a certain tension in the air. I'm not sure if it's sexual or loathing. Perhaps a little of both.

The one thing I'm sure of is that I loathe how much I still want to have sex with him.

Chapter 12

Ash

"I'm just saying you were kind of a jerk."

I stare at Oliver. We're eating Thai food at the counter of my apartment downtown. I need it for the days I'm working extremely late or know I'm going to be drinking. Otherwise, I would have driven into the lake on the way to Wilmette by now.

Oliver has just informed me I should have been nicer to Rye. I'm trying my best to keep my cool and not let him know anything might be amiss between Rye and me. "When was I a jerk?"

"I don't know. The whole time? Look, I see you as a jerk on the day to day. It's rare that you're like... cold to someone."

I raise my eyebrows and drop my chopsticks into my pad Thai. "Cold? I don't think I was *cold*."

"Whatever. That's how it came off. She kept looking at you like you were about to snap at her or something."

Rye kept looking at me. I shouldn't like the sound of that. But I do. I love that she kept looking at me. "Well, I didn't snap, did I?"

Oliver shakes his head through a sip of Sapporo. "Not my point."

"Then what *is* your point?"

"I don't know. She's just a kid."

"You're younger than her."

"Yeah! And I'm just a kid."

I can't help but chuckle. Being in your twenties does still feel like being a kid. Although by that time, I'd already had three kids of my own, so that feeling went away faster. "So what, you don't think she's pretty?" I ask.

Oliver's eyes widen. "I think she's beautiful."

"But you just said she's a kid, so—"

"To you! To you she's a kid. To me she's... " Oliver clicks his tongue and looks away. "I'm not interested."

I grimace. "Alright, then."

"You didn't tell me it was a setup."

"It wasn't, I was just *curious*." This is a half-truth. I couldn't face Rye by myself. It was cowardly, I'll admit it. But there was a small part of me that thought I could maybe... divert her attention onto Oliver. He deserves it. And Rye is a great girl. I've learned as much over the past four months. She's smart and witty. She's got big things ahead of her with her flower shop and...

If I can make her even more off-limits, then I'm sure I won't want her anymore. If I had seen her alone, I wouldn't have been able to hold back. All the thoughts I've had about her over the past months, the way I've missed her body against mine. I can still feel it as if it were just this morning. Her warmth and her curves nestling into the contours of my body.

She's driving me insane.

"I didn't realize I was being a jerk," I say with finality.

Oliver smiles askew. "I know."

I pick up a packet of soy sauce and toss it at him. It hits him square in the forehead.

"Hey!"

"That's what you get for calling your dad a jerk!"

We enjoy the rest of our dinner, moving off the subject of Rye and trying so hard not to talk about work, but unable to avoid it. We're installing new cyber security protocols after several major data breaches in our industry and Oliver's been working overtime to make sure everything goes off without a hitch.

At nine, I'm yawning my ass off. Oliver teases me, "Okay, old man. Bed time," and I resist tossing another soy sauce packet at him.

Once Oliver heads to his own apartment, I do my nightly routine. It's become a bit ritualistic. I take a shower, I put on my moisturizers and serums, do my stretches (okay, maybe I am getting old). And then I settle into bed, debating if I should watch a show or read or...

Fuck. Rye is on my mind. I stare at the ceiling and clench and unclench my fists. Maybe I really was a jerk. Maybe I owe her an apology.

That's as good an excuse as any, right?

I grab my phone off my nightstand, pull up her contact and stare at the number. A quick call. Just to say sorry and that it was nice to see her. No, I can't say that. She might read into it and think I'm trying to get into her pants again.

Fuck it. Rip off the band aid.

I tap the call button and bring the phone to my ear. It rings and rings and rings and I'm starting to think that I've been saved by the god of millennials who don't like to talk on the phone until—

"Hi... " Rye answers, her voice uneasy and almost a question.

"Rye. It's Ash."

"I know. Your name comes up on the screen."

Right. Of course. I just was trying to be polite. "You have a minute?"

I hear her shift wherever she is. I wonder if she's sitting in the family room with Giselle and Clay or in the kitchen making an evening cup of tea or already in bed maybe doing the same thing I am. I wonder what she's wearing.

Ash, you are going to hell.

"Yeah, what's up? Is something wrong?"

"No. Well, yes, but not—basically, I think I owe you an apology for how I acted today."

A pause. "Oh."

"I just... you know I wanted to keep things cordial and I think I might have been a bit of a jerk, so... I'm sorry about that. You don't deserve that."

Rye hesitates before replying, "It's okay. You weren't a jerk."

She's lying. I can sense it. Trying to be nice and make me feel better. "Well, in case I was, I just wanted to apologize. So, I apologize."

"Thank you."

"And I promise, I really did just fuck up the lighting thing. It wasn't meant to be petty or offensive."

Rye laughs lightly. "Good to know. I was wondering if maybe you were trying to get one over on me."

"No, never. Never. I promise. The ecru, though... "

She laughs louder. I'm glad I can still make her laugh. Maybe we can just be friends. "You'll never *ever* get ecru, Ash."

Ash. The echo of the way she said my name in bed remains. *Ashhhh.* She lingered on the 'sh' as if she was trying to hold onto a cloud, knowing it would never be strong enough to keep her. "How are things otherwise? Aside from the wedding?" I regret it as soon as I ask it. Because I know I'll keep her on the phone as long as she lets me.

"Good. They're good. I've been playing around with some arrangement concepts."

"Do you have pictures? I'd love to see them."

"Ummm, sure!"

In just a couple seconds, my phone buzzes with a text message. I put her on speaker. Three different versions of flower arrangements. They're all stunning, all emphasizing a different color. Purple, blue, yellow. "Wow, Rye. These are amazing."

She giggles. "Thank you."

"Seriously. I don't know how you do it."

"Oh, just practice."

I lick my lower lip. I want this guilty feeling to go away. But we've already broken the seal. Is it possible to make things worse just by talking? "Walk me through them, would you?"

I hear her smile over the phone. "Sure."

I hang on every word she says. And from there conversation spirals from thing to thing. Easy. Before we both know it, it's nearly midnight. I'm not tired, not a bit. I could keep talking to her all night. "Can I call you tomorrow?" I ask after we decide to hang up.

"I'd like that."

"Me too."

Rye pauses and then says in her sweetest, sultriest voice, "Goodnight."

My mouth goes numb. I don't reply before she hangs up. I press the phone to my chest. And for the first time in a month, I feel like she's here with me. Right where she belongs.

Chapter 13

Rye

"How fancy is this dinner party going to be, do you think?"

I smile. "You're the one who sets the standard, Ash."

Ash guffaws over the phone. "What do you mean?"

"Um, it's no contest that you'll be the richest person at the table."

He clicks his tongue; with the phone up to my ear, I can hear it clearly. "That really doesn't matter. I'm asking *you*. You're setting the standard."

"Oh, I am, am I?" I ask.

"I default to you, Rye. I always do."

Two weeks since we last saw each other. Two weeks since he called me late at night to apologize to me and we talked and talked until I could barely keep my eyes open. And nearly every night since, I've spoken to Ash on the phone. It's been innocent. Mostly. Hard to keep it entirely innocent when you know how someone feels inside you. It's always in the back of my mind as I hear his voice.

We talk about our days. We talk about the wedding.

And then we just talk about everything else too. I've heard so much about his sons and he's heard all about my friends in Madison and my old job. I've told him about my dreams for the flower shop and he's talked about wanting to learn how to sail. We talked about astrology and I did his birth chart for him. Scorpio. Makes sense.

It's so easy to talk to him when we're not face to face.

A week ago, Giselle and Dad decided they wanted to have a dinner with the wedding party for us to reveal all the details of the wedding to them. I'm about to demand them for compensation because this wedding planning thing has been no fucking joke. I'm just riding it out until the end. Then I can put all my energy to the flower shop. Just have to remind myself that's what is on the other side. The funds for the flower shop. Late at night, I'll go through storefronts available for rent and get all dreamy eyed. Andersonville, Ravenswood, Bucktown... so many options.

I can't wait.

But anyway. The dinner. Tomorrow night.

"What are *you* going to wear?" Ash asks.

This question is so nearly, "What are you wearing right now?" and I sort of wish it was. Of course, the answer I have is some old gray sweats and a T-shirt with the Madison Badger on the front. "Hm. I don't know. A dress probably."

"What color? We can match."

"You're ridiculous," I say through a chuckle.

Ash hums. "Please, it'd be cute. We'll be matching at the wedding anyway."

I cast a look over at my closet, the door slightly ajar. "I don't know. Maybe blue."

"Blue... gotcha."

"Please don't show up in blue."

"I'm going to wear blue."

I groan and hear Ash laugh over the phone. He certainly can act like a dad to me sometimes. I almost like him more for it.

"I'm just teasing. I won't wear blue. Promise."

* * *

As promised, Ash shows up at dinner not in blue but in a beautiful, forest green suit. No tie, thank god. Otherwise, this would go from a business casual dinner to like a formal thing and I'm not prepared for that in my cobalt, eyelet fabric sun dress.

I'm already talking with other members of the wedding party when he arrives out on the patio. We have a gorgeous fenced-in yard which is hard to come by in Lincoln Park. A small garden, a dark wooden deck with a glass topped table for hosting, and a little fire pit that used ever so rarely, but still, completes the vibe.

When he walks in, I only allow myself to observe him out of the corner of my eye. He immediately greets my father with a hug and Giselle with a kiss on the cheek. If he wants to look at me, he doesn't. It's better that way.

I move my focus away from Ash and back to the conversation I'm having about Nepali wedding customs with Giselle's coworker, Celia, the bridesmaid.

"Of course, most women don't wear sindoor powder in their hair nearly as much. Mostly saved for special occasions. But the representation of marriage as a physical change is something you don't think about," Celia says, blinking at me behind her thick rimmed black glasses. "Many cultures have rings, others have clothing, et cetera. And as we modernize, we are shedding this as a signifier of how to identify who is who in our culture. What do you think that means?"

I feel his eyes on me. Just his gaze alone sets my body alight. Fuck. Not here. Not now. And never again. "What do *I* think it means? I don't know."

Celia leans in closer to me, eager. "Hazard a guess."

"Well, as women why should we be identified by our relationship status?"

Celia touches her nose. "Exactly. But at the same time, isn't our relationship status a protection? A way to signify who can and cannot approach?"

"To be honest, I never want to be approached," I say with a dry laugh.

Celia does not find this funny, which is why I'm relieved when I feel a soft touch to my shoulder.

I know the hand, know every curve of it. "Excuse me for interrupting."

I turn to find myself face to face with Ash. He's smiling down at me in a way that is unreadable. Neither too excited, nor unexcited. Placid. "Good to see you, Rye."

"Hi, Ash," I say. I ignore the slight pull inside me to wrap my arms around him in a hug. Over the phone I've felt so close to him. But he's still at a distance. "This is Celia Collins. She works in the same department as Giselle. She's a bridesmaid."

"Ashton Hawthorn," he says, extending his hand to her. "Best Man."

Celia smiles uneasily and takes his hand. "Pleasure to meet you. Tell me, what are your thoughts on the cultural tradition of—"

"Listen, Celia, I need to speak with Ash privately before dinner, forgive me for tearing him away," I say with an irritated smile and yank Ash to an unoccupied space on the deck where we can be alone.

"Easy," he says with a laugh. "You've got a grip like an iron vice."

"Trust me, I'm doing you a favor. She's been talking to me for the past hour about the anthropological impacts of marriage traditions around the world."

Ash's eyebrows jump. "An hour? I thought the party started half an hour ago. Am I that late?"

"She got here *early*," I say in a whisper.

Ash's lips bubble, holding back a laugh.

"Don't laugh. I've been miserable."

"I'm glad to have been your excuse to get away from her, then."

I realize I'm still touching his arm. Both of our eyes fall to my grip on his bicep. I release him with a nervous laugh and clasp my hands in front of the skirty of my dress. "Anyway. It's good to see you."

"You too," Ash says. He looks to the rest of the party and, without returning his gaze to me, says, "You look nice."

"Yes, even better since you didn't match with me."

Ash grins. "Green and blue are at the very least related."

Related. Yes. A great word for how we should treat each other. As if we're related. Off-limits. Incestuous. Wrong.

"Both cool colors," he adds.

I nod. "Are you ready for this evening?"

"Oh, of course. This is low stakes."

I widen my eyes. "Low stakes?!"

"Relative to what I do every day, yeah," he says, charmed by my corporate innocence. "Relax, Rye. They're going to love it."

"Hope so," I swallow. For Giselle not wanting her

wedding to be a huge thing, this sure feels like a lot of people. Tonight, those in attendance are the wedding party members and their significant others. In total, twelve people will be at the table, including Ash and me. It's not like presenting a Ted Talk or anything (which Ash has done and I'm ashamed to say I have watched it more than once), but it's more presenting than I've done since college. Flowers aren't nearly as judgmental as people.

"Seriously, Rye. They're going to love it. All they asked is we plan them a wedding. We took it seriously, we did the work, we... " he trails off and swallows. "They're going to love it."

"There you two are! Wow, what a handsome pair!" Giselle squeals as she comes over to us. She touches both of our arms, forming a little circle. "Now, you two can't look this nice at the wedding or else you'll upstage me and Clay."

We both laugh nervously and exchange a look.

"We're going to sit down for dinner in a minute. Your dad's just obsessing over the ratatouille and—"

"As usual," Ash and I both say simultaneously.

Giselle's eyes widen. "Okay. That was weird." She waves her hand as if clearing smoke. "Anyway, so we'll be ready in a minute. And then we'll eat and during dessert, you're up."

"Can you tell Rye that she has nothing to worry about? Your Maid of Honor is worried sick that we're going to disappoint you or something?" Ash says, touching my back the slightest bit.

I do everything in my power not to react as if I'm being prodded with a hot fire poker.

"Oh my god. Rye! Why are you worried?"

"That's what I said," Ash answers.

Giselle wraps her arms around me. I can smell the

champagne. She's already had three glasses. I know she was nervous about tonight too. Not because of me, but because the whole wedding *thing* has made her nervous beyond compare. There's a reason she wanted to elope. "Rye. You're perfect. Everything you do."

"Did someone say ratatouille?" my dad calls out from the doorway onto the deck from the kitchen and the gawking excitement of dinner commencing is enough to calm my nerves for a moment.

That is until Ash and I make our way to the table and notice that Giselle has placed our place cards beside one another. Neither of us is willing to make a spectacle. But if Ash's heart is beating as fast as mine just from sitting next to him, we definitely have a problem.

Chapter 14

Ash

I didn't know that Clay was not only a competent chef, but a pastry chef as well. Dessert is a spread of some of the finest looking French pastries I've ever seen on this side of the Atlantic.

"He's been working all day on them," Rye murmurs in my ear.

I get goosebumps when her breath hits my face. Despite our proximity during the meal, we've spoken very little to one another, over-correcting for our past indiscretions. People are going to start wondering if we don't like each other if we continue this dedication to distance.

Even though she hasn't been talking to me most of the meal, I haven't been able to get my mind off of her. Right there sitting beside me in her blue dress, I think of all the things I want to do to her. I catch glimpses of her thighs from time to time as she shifts in her seat, the eyelet material serving as a way for me to peek behind the curtain.

I have a great view into the neckline of her dress that leaves little to the imagination. Not that I *need* to imagine. I remember the tender buds of her nipples and the milky skin of her breasts, how perfectly they felt in my hands, my mouth, up against my bare chest.

I would have been hard most of the meal if I hadn't been sitting directly across from her father, my best friend. That's a boner killer for sure, one that I desperately need. Every time I've dipped toward horniness, Clay suddenly says something like, "Ash! Ash, tell me, did you ever replace the coffee machine in the breakroom or does it still sound like a dying toad?" or "Ashton, the boys: they're coming to the wedding, right?" or "Let me see pictures of Piper. I'll live vicariously through you." That last one garnered a glower from Rye I'd never want to be on the end of.

Now, it's dessert. And, as Giselle informed us, it's time for "the presentation." I have to laugh at the melodrama of it. Rye goes to retrieve her planner, although she's switched out the black plastic binder for a frilly, cream colored one with bows and things. I wonder if she's decorated it herself. I would not be surprised.

"You ready?" I ask as she takes her seat again.

"No," she says dryly. "I don't even know where to start."

I watch her flip through the sections of the binder. I could conjure a plan in no time flat. I already have ideas of how best to dispel the information. I just have years of practice of not only convincing people that my ideas are good, but making them believe without question I'm right.

"Just start at the beginning. Tell the story of how the night will go."

Rye's hands are shaking. Fuck, she's really nervous. I touch her wrist delicately and her eyes shoot into mine. Crisp, anxious blue, like waves trembling before a storm. I feel a pang in my heart. Sure, I want her. But I also care for her. I really do. I can't stand to see her like this.

Before I can say anymore words of encouragement,

Giselle claps her hands and gleefully announces, "Okay! Everyone grab a pastry and listen up. Our Maid of Honor and Best Man have a presentation."

I draw my hand away from Rye reflexively. She blinks, scanning the table, and then opens her binder to the very first page. Stares at it. The whole table is silent. The world is silent. All of us waiting for Rye to speak.

"So, um, first I want to thank my dad and Giselle for giving me the opportunity to plan the wedding. And Ash for... um... "

"I'm nothing but a glorified assistant, I assure you," I say playfully to the table. They chuckle in response. I glance at Clay and Giselle who are holding hands plainly on the table for everyone to see. They are both wearing big, hopeful smiles.

Rye shakes her head. "You're much more than that. You're the one who fought tooth and nail for ecru napkins. That counts for something."

More laughter. We exchange a smile and in that moment I see Rye step into her confidence. She brushes her beautiful dark hair over her shoulder and puffs her chest. "Picture this. It's September eighteenth. Morning. And it's sixty-eight degrees, at least according to the Farmer's Almanac it will be..."

And from there, the spark sets everything alight. My god, does she tell the story. With very little help or assistance from me, mind you. The wedding party is held captive, not least the bride and groom who are captivated by everything Rye says. When she talks about the wedding band, I can't help but chime in with an anecdote about meeting them: "We couldn't keep from dancing. Seriously. And you know I usually need to be drunk to do that."

"I'm not sure if your moves would be better or worse," Rye teases and again, more laughter.

She is something else. *We* are something else. I can't deny that. Through all of the ups and downs, the coldness, the sleeping together, the phone calls we've had every night for two weeks that I know we shouldn't have, we have really put together a day that's going to be so fucking special.

By the end of the presentation, there's not a dry eye. I hate to think about the wedding if everyone's already getting choked up at Rye just telling them about the color scheme. But that's Rye. "At times, it's been hellish. Not to mention what a pain in my ass he can be," she says, jabbing my arm with her pointer finger.

"Hey! Everyone needs a devil's advocate when it comes to wedding planning."

She grins at me. Even though she beams, it's like it's just for me. I capture it in my memory. Maybe I can survive off that the rest of my life.

"But it's been my greatest honor to plan this for you two. And I hope you like it," Rye finishes and then leans on her elbows, bashfully tucking her face behind her hands. "That's it."

The table erupts in applause and excitement. Giselle's crying and Clay is on the verge of tears. "I need a fucking drink," Clay announces and everyone agrees.

There is a flurry of hugging and kissing and congratulating and handshaking. Clay comes to me and pats my arm before engulfing me in a hug. "What did I do to deserve you, huh?"

I nearly laugh. I don't know what bad thing he did to deserve a friend who slept with his daughter. Who still thinks about sleeping with his daughter. "I've been happy to, Clay," I say, before letting him retreat to Giselle's side again.

Everyone settles back into dessert, except for Rye, who has her binder clasped tight to her chest and looks like she's just seen a ghost.

"You alright?" I ask with a frown.

Rye snaps out of her trance and blushes. "Oh, yeah. Yeah, totally. I just... Need a moment, I think. Bathroom, or... Yeah."

She gets to her feet and scrambles back into the house. No one seems to notice but me. Giselle and Clay are cooing to each other, staring in each other's eyes. The rest of the wedding party is indulging in champagne and desserts.

I could follow her. Would anyone question it? Would anyone miss me? Even if they did, what would they think? We were just debriefing or unwinding or decompressing. Right?

Logic is not on my side, and soon I find myself rising from my seat to follow her. However, she's not in the half-bath off the kitchen. I check the bathroom off the guest bedroom at the back of the first floor, the one I spent many nights in when Rose passed away and I needed to be close to friends and then returned to only a few years later to be with Clay to make the house not feel so empty. Not there either.

She must be upstairs. I carefully climb the staircase and look around. I don't know if I've ever been up here other than an initial tour the very first time I visited the Linden house. I hear running water and follow the sound down the hall to a door that's very nearly closed but not quite. I knock softly. "Rye?"

The water shuts off and then silence.

"It's me. It's Ash, I just wanted to check on you."

The door squeaks open; Rye backs up against the bathroom wall and lets out a heavy sigh. She looks like she's been crying.

"Hey… " I say softly, approaching her as I would a scared cat. "What's up? Why are you crying?"

Rye wipes her face clear of any trace of tears. "I don't know." She laughs to herself. "I just couldn't help it."

I smile.

"Thank you for checking on me. But I'm fine, you really don't have to—"

"No, I wanted to," I say in a low, emphatic voice.

Her eyes flick up to mine and then away. She crosses her arms over her chest making her breasts swell slightly at the neckline of her dress. Fuck. "I can't stop thinking about my mom."

I furrow my brow and nod. "That makes sense."

"Like I'm so happy for them and I'm also so sad."

"I know that feeling."

Our eyes meet. Beyond everything, we've always both shared the knowledge of loss. We've both been gutted and know what it is to yearn for love you can no longer have.

Fuck, it's so perverse but I want her. I want her so bad.

I bridge the gap between comfort and desire by touching her shoulder softly. She doesn't draw away, giving into my touch easily, her eyes shutting. A tear rolls down her face.

Why is she so beautiful when she cries?

"Can I hug you?"

"Yes, please," she replies without hesitating. She throws herself into my arms and buries her face against my chest. Her hands slide up my back to my shoulder blades.

It takes me a moment to settle around her. I didn't expect her to meet my offer with such fullness. Now that she has, I'm going to relish every moment. I hold her to me as tight as I can, resting my chin on top of her head. I could die like this.

When I'm alone, the guilt is hard to endure. The guilt of lusting after my best friend's daughter. The guilt of maybe finding love somewhere other than Rose. But when Rye is right here in my arms, there is no guilt. There is only the overwhelming feeling that this is exactly how we are supposed to be.

"It's okay," I whisper into her hair. Without thinking, I move my hands up her back to the back of her head as I would comforting Piper.

Rye lets her head fall back into my hands. She looks up with me with glossy, red-rimmed eyes. Her lips are puffy and scarlet, her face sticky with tears, and yet there's still something in me chanting, *Kiss her, kiss her, kiss her*.

Suddenly, her lips perk in a small smile and her eyes have a glimmer of something. A hope. A wish. I know that look. I saw it a little over a month ago. When I had her.

Fuck it.

I kiss her. Rougher than I intend, immediately delving my tongue between her lips. I can't help but let her know how much I want her, how intensely.

Rye's fingers dig into my back, pulling me into her. This kiss is welcomed. It's needed.

We both need this.

"I'm sorry," I say breathlessly between kisses, but the apology is only in word, not in action. I'm not stopping my lips from devouring her.

"Don't be," she replies.

I move my lips to her neck, nipping the skin without concern if I leave a mark. I'm not thinking with my head, I'm thinking with my hardening dick. Might regret it later, but not right now. Now, my mind is entirely on the subject of having Rye. Every part of her.

She lets out a whimper and slips her hands under my green suit jacket to my waist with such voracity that my shirt comes untucked. This is happening. Again.

"Tell me to stop," I say, sliding my hands down to her curvaceous ass and pulling her pelvis to meet mine. A wave of euphoria shoots up my body and makes my skin hot.

"No," Rye replies.

"Tell me," I say. My hips subtly pulse into hers. I can't help it.

She shakes her head. "No," she repeats and starts to work the buttons on my shirt until most of my chest is uncovered.

"Shit, Rye, tell me to stop or else I'll do something stupid."

Rye snakes her hand up my neck and grabs a handful of my hair, pulling slightly. She raises her lips as close to my Adam's apple as she can get. "*Do it*," she says.

Those two words send my primal instincts into overdrive. I can't deny her. As if I ever would.

I kiss her harshly again and push her up against the sink, grinding my hips against hers. Rye runs her hands up my chest, thumbing my nipples.

I'm not thinking about the people downstairs. Her father. His future wife. Their friends. They're all so far away. The only thing in the world is Rye and me. I like the sound of that.

"Can't stop thinking about you," I say, sloppily dropping my face to her bare cleavage, skimming the swells of her breasts with my lips. "Need you."

"Need... " she repeats as if it's an incantation and forces her hand into my pants, grabbing a handful of me.

I gasp as she jerks my cock. "Fuck, Rye. Fuck." Her grip has the perfect amount of force in it to tease me, make me want more.

I put my hand on her cheek and curl my thumb into her mouth. Rye's lips tighten around it, her eyes rolling up to meet mine. She sucks on it, swirls her tongue around it. All I can imagine is her doing that to my cock, so swollen in her hand I'm afraid I might burst from a hand job alone.

"Look at you. Pretty mouth. Pretty everything."

Rye smiles and hums, leaning back against the bathroom counter. She releases me to bunch up the skirt of her dress up, further and further, until the tops of her thighs are exposed. I lick my lips, salivating as I remember the way that she tasted all those weeks ago. Her tang, her sweetness. Unforgettable.

I follow her hands with mine, running them up the thickness of her thighs to her hips where the band of a tiny thong sits. "Show me your panties," I say barely audible.

Rye smiles mischievously and raises the skirt further, all the way up. A pair of lacy red panties hides her lower lips. They're darker right at the center. She's wet. So wet already.

"Mmm. Wow."

She giggles. "You like them? They're for you."

I bite my lower lips and nod. "Like them a lot. Thank you." In a quick motion, I undo my pants and release my cock. It bobs out, hungry and ready. I feel the weight of my need for her in my balls, heavy with seed.

Rye starts to shift back onto the counter, but I stop her. "No, no. Turn around. Want to show you how beautiful you are when I fuck you."

Her eyes widen, but she follows my instruction, turning around, swaying her ass as a temptation to me.

"Good girl," I say and then hike up her dress, revealing her beautiful bottom. I pull her panties down, catching a glimpse of her in the mirror. She's looking back at me demurely, almost nervous. "I've got you, Rye," I say reassuringly.

She smiles; her eyes raise to meet mine in the mirror. "I know you do."

I want to be tender with her and care for her just as much as I want to fuck her. I'm totally doomed. I shift my hips forward, sliding into the crevice of her beautiful center. Rye's head drops back and her lips part. Her lipstick is totally gone now, chin rubbed raw by the scruff on my face. Dear god, this is going to be hard to cover up.

"You're so wet for me, baby."

All she can do is smile as the head of my cock bumps up against her clit. Enough with this hesitation. I'm going in.

I find the perfect angle; Rye shifts her hips back toward me, inviting me in about halfway. Her gasp of pain and pleasure keeps me grounded. Got to go slow, stretch her out. Don't want to hurt her. I pulse my hips slow.

"Harder," Rye says. "All the way."

My attempt at restraint is totally dashed when she slams her hips back against me, taking almost my entire length. "Holy shit," I sputter.

"We don't have much time, so fuck me, Ash, fuck me," Rye nearly begs. I'm not going to say no to that.

"Oh, I'll fuck you good, baby," I growl and drop my mouth to her ear before thrusting my whole length inside of her. Rye squeals; I cup her mouth in my hand and whisper, "I'm going to fuck you so good."

Her eyes rolls back as I work. Stroke after stroke, pushing my whole length into her. I don't know what brings me more pleasure: her reactions or her tight pussy.

Together, they're making me insatiable. I wrap my hand around the nape of her neck and stand up, fucking her with intense force.

Rye clutches the lip of the counter, knuckles going white. My name stumbles out of her mouth again and again, too clouded to find anything else to say. And I'm not complaining. The repetition of my name heightens the swells of pleasure inside me.

I start to play with her clit, watching her reaction in the mirror.

"Oh my god, *Ashton.*"

"Watch. Look at how I'm playing with you."

Her eyes move to my fingers dancing around her clit. They tremble. "What are you *doing to me*?"

"You close?"

Rye tries to respond with words, but all that comes out is a limp moan. She's close. And I'm close.

I'm not wearing a condom.

"You come and I'll pull out," I say hoarsely.

She shakes her head.

"Rye."

"Come inside."

I just lost my last brain cell. My balls are tight as drums and at the sound of that, they twitch, knowing what's in store. "Are you—" I can barely keep my composure to ask. "Are you *sure*?"

Rye bucks her hips hard against me. Her eyes meet mine in the mirror. "Come inside me," she repeats, eyes as steady as sapphires.

What comes next is nearly impossible for me to account for. I press myself into her as far as I will go and pull her hips tight to me. I don't have any room to move, but I jerk and rut as hard as possible. Rye bounces on my cock, head lolling to the side, a moan hiccupping out of her.

I'm climbing higher and higher. I can't hold it in. I pinch her clit hard and her eyes burst open, jaw hanging. She's coming. Her pussy clenches around me. I can't hold it in.

I come inside her. I bury my face in her shoulder to muffle a jerky yelp. I keep coming. There's so much, I can't stop.

Rye wraps a hand around the back of my head, stroking my hair. "That's it," she coos. "Let it go."

I hold her close to me until I feel myself unstiffening. Finally. I'm not sure how long it took. "Holy shit, Rye," I whisper and then kiss the side of her head.

Rye leans back into me. I look at this picture in the mirror. Sure, we're a fucking mess. Frazzled and sweaty, clothing mussed, hair a wreck. And yet, at the same time, I can see that she fits so perfectly in my arms. It's not just a feeling. It looks right too.

I trail kisses down her hairline and she lets out a sated giggle. "I'll get Plan B tomorrow morning," she says. "I promise."

For the briefest second, I want to tell her *don't*. For the briefest second, I want her to know that the thought of our bodies merging together and creating a child would be the most perfect thing in the world. For the briefest second, I want her to know that I want her forever.

That second passes and those thoughts are replaced with one overwhelming thought: "We need to get cleaned up. Fast."

Chapter 15

Rye

I stare at the Plan B behind the pharmacist. It sits up on the shelf like it's taunting me. I came into Walgreen's thinking this would be a quick and easy transaction, but something has just hit me like a ton of bricks.

I'm late.

Like. Two weeks late.

I'm never late. My periods are extremely regular and have been my whole life thank *god*. Every twenty-eight days, just as *The Care and the Keeping of You* told me it would be.

Calm down, Rye. You've been so stressed. That can prevent a period.

It can. But the alternate explanation is louder and scarier.

You and Ash fucked (for the first time) seven weeks ago.

And I might have been drinking wine, but I'm not drunk enough to not remember we didn't use condoms. I would have remembered the smell of the latex and the feeling of him being sheathed inside me like that.

No, we did it completely raw and unprotected.

I hadn't even thought about it until now. I was too caught up in the guilt of it even having happened to think about any other consequences than being a bad person. Holy fucking shit.

"Are you okay?"

I snap out of my haze. The pharmacist, a small woman with silver hair, blinks at me from behind her thick glasses. "Um. Yes. Sorry. I just... never mind."

I walk away from the pharmacy counter in a daze. This was just supposed to be a quick trip before I ran Giselle's dress to the tailor and then met with my dad for lunch at the restaurant we're having catering their wedding. Pop in some Plan B and have lunch with my dad. What girl hasn't done that in their life?

Although, most people aren't fucking their dad's best friends.

I get back into my car and immediately panic. Why didn't I just grab a pregnancy test? I was right fucking there? But I can't go back in, that'd be so embarrassing. And a pregnancy test doesn't really tell you for sure, you need to get the blood work to confirm.

I don't have a gynecologist in Chicago anymore. I haven't even thought about finding new doctors to replace the ones I had in Madison. It's a fucking Saturday. No gynecologist is open on a Saturday and if they are, those appointments are probably booked weeks in advance. Jesus Christ. How could I be such an idiot?

Miraculously, though, I have a referral Giselle gave me months ago for her gyno. I call and there's an appointment available if I can come in right away. It was meant to be.

I speed across town to get there. I hold onto the steering wheel with a vice grip. How could I have been so stupid? How could I have neglected such a key piece of what *sex* is?

For fucks sake, I asked Ash to come inside me last night as if I was this untouchable little nymph who could grab some Plan B and terminate a pregnancy before it even happened.

As I sit in the waiting room at the gynecologist's office, I can't help but stare at the women around me. Some of them aren't pregnant, but some of them are. They all look like this is just a normal day. A normal pregnant day. I can't imagine being used to being pregnant. However, these women probably all planned their pregnancies with their husbands and are probably looking forward to spending their six week maternity leaves away from their offices.

I can't be pregnant. I'm way too young. Except I'm not. I'm twenty-nine. Almost thirty. That's not too young. But I *feel* too young. I don't even have a husband or boyfriend. I've got a sperm donor.

And it's Ashton fucking Hawthorn.

I do some deep breaths. *Keep calm, Rye. We don't know for sure. Not yet.* It's possible I'm *not* pregnant. Maybe I just haven't measured my cycle right. Maybe I'm not late at all, just stressed. Just forgetful.

I play through the events of the night before in my head to calm myself down. I know it doesn't make sense to think of Ash when he's part of the reason I'm so stressed, but the way he made me feel when he came to find me, when he hugged me and comforted me when I was crying about my mom...

I haven't been filled with that level of comfort and warmth in a long time.

After we did what we did in my bathroom, we both got cleaned up, checking one another to make sure there were no signs of what had happened between us. It was tender and sweet, him smoothing out wrinkles in my dress, me running my fingers through his hair to make sure it didn't look soiled.

Ash decided he would go down first and let my dad know that I was crying. It would be a good cover. He could play up that he was just caring for me in the time he'd been gone.

Of course, what kind of care, my dad would never know. Hopefully never, at least.

And before he left me there in the bathroom, to my total shock, he kissed me. Softly. Right on the lips. So different from the goodbye after our first encounter, the awkward one in his kitchen where he denied any further connection.

Though wordless, it felt like a promise of more. I dreamt about him all night.

A nurse in blue scrubs comes out from a little hall and calls out my name. "Rye Linden?"

I stand, holding my purse subconsciously across my belly. If I'm pregnant, I'm not going to be showing for a while thank god. I don't even know if I'll keep it. But I can't help the impulse. Almost like a maternal instinct.

I follow her inside, tell her everything going on, and when I tell her how long it's been since my period, her eyebrows raise in such a way that nearly confirms the pregnancy before she runs any tests.

I go pee in a cup and hand it off through the strange metal door in the bathroom that always makes me feel like I'm a prisoner in an industrial jail handing off an empty bowl of gruel. And then back to the examination room where I'm to wait for the doctor.

I am determined to make a decision before I know the answer. I can't have a baby. I'm unestablished and unpartnered. I'm in no place to be a mother.

The doctor comes in a little later with her clipboard

tucked against her chest; she looks to be around my age which makes me feel entirely unaccomplished, and has beautiful olive skin and dark, plaited hair. "Rye?"

"Yeah, that's me."

"Hi, I'm Doctor Uri. Thanks for coming in today. How are you feeling?"

I swallow and try to smile pleasantly. "Nervous."

Dr. Uri smiles. "I understand. Well, I'll get to it. Your urine sample does indeed suggest that you're pregnant."

My heart sinks. It must be visible on my face because she doesn't wait for my response. "We can do some bloodwork to confirm. That won't come in for a few days, unfortunately, since we have to send it out to a lab. But we can do a transvaginal ultrasound which should give us abundant information so you can walk out of here with all the information you need."

"Sounds good," I say, zipping my legs together just as I did when I watched the *Miracle of Life* video in sex ed at fourteen.

I end up on my back, with my feet propped up at the end of the table, the blue paper cover across my lap as if the doctor *isn't* going to be looking at my genitals. Dr. Uri prepares the wand; she puts a condom on it and lubes it up before gently sliding it inside me. Her eyes are trained to the screen attached to the cart of equipment, surreptitiously turned away from me so I can't see if anything is wrong or right or what. I wouldn't know what to look for if it hit me in the face.

"Okay, that looks good," she says to herself.

I raise my eyebrows. What looks good? That I'm maybe *not* carrying a baby?

As if hearing my thoughts, Dr. Uri turns her gaze to me and smiles sympathetically. "You're pregnant."

No thoughts. Just feelings. Tears pricking my eyes. I'm not sure if it's a good feeling or a bad one. I'm just overwhelmed

She turns the screen toward me and starts to point to different blobs on the screen that don't look much like a baby at all. Her finger articulates to a place on the screen so small and subtle. "That's your baby."

It's not just a baby. It's Ashton Hawthorn's baby. And that does it. The waterworks commence. I sob into my hands. Dr. Uri is incredibly kind, although unable to read my reaction as good or bad. "There are options, Rye, there are options."

I don't need options. I know. Seeing it was all I needed to know that even though I don't have things together on paper, I can do this. My baby might have been conceived under a cloak of forbidden desire. But there's nothing wrong about the result. It's beautiful. A baby... my baby...

I never knew how much I needed this.

After the tears are dried and Dr. Uri and I laugh over my reaction, she gives me all the information I need, gives me a rundown on my next steps, what I should expect in the next few weeks, and when I should come in next to see her. I ask her not to mention anything to Giselle should she see her and she doesn't bat an eye. "Of course not, I'd never discuss your business with another patient."

I can tell we will be good friends. She's the only other person but me that knows about what's happening inside me. I trust her implicitly. I wish I could hug her, but I think that might be inappropriate.

Of course, it is not all sunshine and roses. I'm going to have Ashton Hawthorn's baby. My *dad's best friend's baby*. A man who is seventeen years older than me who has only ever loved me in secret. Surely, he couldn't be a part of this with me.

Could he be? Would he be?

I won't know if I don't tell him. And regardless of his response, which I hope upon hope is full of love for me and our baby (our baby!!), he deserves to know.

Once I'm in the car, I give my dad a call. "Daddy, I have to cancel our lunch. I'm so sorry."

"Why? What's going on?"

"I have a... a last minute meeting," I say and then immediately follow up, "A florist in the city. Someone I've respected for a while. Wants to look at my portfolio."

My dad gasps. "Oh! You have to go. You have to. Don't worry about me."

I feel horrible for lying to him, especially considering that he wants nothing more for me than my success and happiness. Of course he wouldn't want me to miss an opportunity for lunch date. Just add this lie to the pile. My worst one yet, honestly. Because now, it's not just lust and hunger.

It's become something so much more than that.

I have to tell Ash that I'm pregnant.

And no matter what, I'm keeping it.

Chapter 16

Ash

My boys all sit around my office in various states of relaxation. Some days are just that way. We all play hooky and hide in my office, shooting the shit and cracking jokes. We'll turn on our "out of office" reply and kick back. Watch a movie, play video games, talk about things that are weighing on our minds.

I love working with my kids.

Today's subject: women. More specifically, dates for Clay's wedding.

"Well, I'm bringing Piper," Jarred says, laid back on the couch, tossing a stress ball overhead and catching it.

The next time he lobs the ball in the air, Oliver snatches it and walks away with a snicker. "Piper's invited, dumbass."

Jarred sits up and huffs with annoyance. "You think I can pay attention to my daughter and a date at a *wedding*? Dream on."

I redirect the conversation to my youngest son. He's knocking back an energy drink and scrolling through Instagram. "Keif? Who are you bringing?"

"June, of course."

"Of course," Jarred and Oliver mimic.

Keifer's eyes finally snap up from the phone. "What?"

"Don't you think you're getting a little old to be dragging around your kindergarten best friend to events?" Jarred says, crossing his arms.

"Do you have a problem with June?" Keifer asks in annoyance.

"Of course I don't have a problem with her," Jarred replies.

I sigh. "Guys..." They're hard on each other, but it's out of love and familiarity.

Jarred goes on, "I'm just saying that she can't be your date forever, that's all. It's like taking your sister if you had one."

Keifer returns to scrolling on his phone, slumping down in his chair. "I'll have more fun with June," he grumbles.

"Okay, Keifer's bringing June!" I announce, effectively ending the discussion. "Oliver?"

Oliver's been picking through a bowl of mixed nuts on the coffee table, taking all the cashews. He turns and flashes me a smug smile. "Flying solo, daddio."

"I could have told you that," Jarred says under his breath. Ever the instigator.

"Do you want to fight, bro?" Oliver asks playfully.

Jarred sighs and puts his hands over his eyes. Something's weighing on him, but if he's not talking about it, I'm not going to pry. I know the heaviness that comes with being a dad. Always worrying.

"Besides, weddings are supposed to be a good place for singles, right?"

"You don't mean to tell me you think you can pick up a girl at Clay's wedding," Keifer dryly says.

Oliver purses his lips and glares. "You don't have to be rude about it. Besides, what about Clay's daughter?"

My insides twist together and I let out an uneasy laugh. "What about her?"

"She single? Maybe you could..." Oliver gestures between him and his brothers. "Make something happen?"

I have to put a lid on the boiling possessiveness inside me. I don't deserve to feel that way. Rye isn't mine. Not now. Not ever. But a part of her has been mine. Our intimate moments together have connected me to her in a way that I could never have expected.

Oliver has a point. She's certainly much more age appropriate for one of the boys. But I'll be damned if I'm going to pass her on to one of my sons, even if I have no idea what's going on between us. "It's going to be an emotional day for her. I don't think she's going to be very interested in *flirting*, Olly."

Oliver bristles at his childhood nickname. "Please, anything but Olly."

"Besides, what makes you think she'd be interested in you, *Olly*?" Jarred taunts, throwing a pillow at Oliver.

Oliver catches it. "Hey!" He launches himself over to the couch and starts to play wrestle with his older brother.

"Boys, come on. Not on the leather!" I cry out but I know it's of no use. They'll have their little spar and then get over it. I chuckle to myself.

"What about you, Dad?" Keifer asks, still staring at his phone.

"Hm?"

His light green eyes dance up to mine. "Are you going to bring a date?"

I suck on the inside of my cheeks. My thoughts race. I'd never considered bringing a date. After all, I don't really *date.* But if I were to have a date, I'd only want it to be one person. And she is totally off-limits. "Um... no. No, I don't think so."

There's a knock at the door. I straighten up in my seat and run a hand through my hair. "Look alive, guys!"

All my sons sit up and try to put on a prim, corporate look. To the outside eye, I think they play the part just fine. But to me, they all look like they're playing dress up in suits and ties. Still my little guys. I take a deep breath. "Come in!"

My secretary, Sandy opens the door. "Sorry, Mr. Hawthorn, I tried to call but you weren't picking up. There's someone here to see you."

"I don't have a meeting until one o'clo... " I begin with a quizzical expression but trail off when I see who is standing behind Sandy. Rye. "Send her in."

Sandy steps aside to let Rye through. How does Rye get more stunning by the day? She's not all made up like she was yesterday and her hair is swept back into a claw clip on the back of her head, but she just glows. Something about her just exudes brilliance at all times.

"Sorry to interrupt you at work," she says with a nervous look to the boys.

"No, not at all," I say, shooting up from my chair. I'm so happy to see her and hope I don't look too eager.

"Rye! Good to see you!" Oliver announces jollily. "Guys, this is Clay's daughter."

Both Jarred and Keifer have the same reaction I had except a bit more visibly, their eyes bugging out of their head, further lending credence to the notion that Rye Linden has changed an awful lot over the past nine years.

"We can do introductions another time. Rye and I have to discuss something for Clay's wedding, if you don't mind giving us a moment," I say, gesturing the boys to the door.

Keifer rolls his eyes and Oliver snorts.

"Guys, come on, keep it professional," I say, smacking them each playfully on their shoulders.

Rye smiles shyly from the corner. "Good to see you all again."

The boys file out the door, saying their goodbyes. Finally, Rye and I are alone in my office.

I have to say, I'm turned on that she'd show up out of the blue like this. For what, I can only guess at, but if my hope is correct, then I'm in for a *fantastic* lunch break.

"Is it alright if I close the door?" she asks meekly.

I twiddle with the button on my suit jacket. "Of course."

Rye turns around to shut the door; I quietly approach her from behind with a confident smile. When she turns, she jumps and clutches her heart, "You scared me!"

"I'm sorry," I say with a chuckle. "I wanted to say hello to you properly." I wrap my hands around her face and kiss her gently. "Hi."

"H-hi... "

"Don't be shy with me, Rye," I say and then kiss her again. The kiss lingers. She's distant. Nervous. It's so endearing. "You're fucking brave to show up here."

She shakes her head, "No, I'm not."

"You kidding? Out of the blue like this?"

"Are you mad?"

I put my hand on her lower back and bring her close to me so our chests touch. "Do I seem mad, honey?"

Her lips curl into a smile. There she is.

"Come on. We have to be quick," I say, engulfing her in my embrace and kissing her deeply. I immediately reach for her ass and squeeze. "Fuck. Can't get enough of your body."

"Ash—"

I giggle childishly, "And the way you say my name! Fuck, you're perfect."

"*Ashton.*"

"Stop, you'll make me come right here," I say.

Rye pulls away from my embrace. "Listen, Ash, we need to—"

"You want me to chase you?" I ask, following her like a puppy. I come up behind her and trail kisses down her neck, following the curve of waist with my hands. "You want me to beg? I will."

She settles for only a moment before unwinding from my embrace again. "I didn't come here for that, Ash," she says, her eyes hardened in mine. "I want to talk to you."

I freeze. Something is wrong. There is an urgency in her voice, a desperation. I've probably left her so confused after last night. She probably wants answers. "I want to talk to you too."

Rye blinks. "Oh."

"I haven't been… " I go to her again, this time tenderly, without the fire of lust bursting from inside me. I run my hands down her arm and hold onto her elbows. "I haven't been able to stop thinking about you. Not just since last night but before that. Before we even… from the moment I saw you all those months ago."

Her brow bends worriedly and her mouth tightens into a thin line.

"Rye," I say her name like it is only for me and wrap her face in my hands. "I know it's impossible. Or it should be. I know it's wrong. But I've been fighting this feeling inside me and I can't anymore."

"Oh god, Ash," she mutters, holding her lips back from a smile.

"I think there's something here. There's a future. I don't know how we go about it or... " I have to take a deep breath to keep my voice from breaking. "I don't just want to hide what I'm feeling in the dead of night or sneak around. I want you, Rye. All of you."

Her lower lip trembles; where I was hoping to see joy is just grimness. Her face grows pale. She almost looks ill.

And then—

"I'm pregnant."

I can't hide my shock. My terror. "What?"

"I'm pregnant," she repeats.

I am transported to the feeling of being seventeen. Looking at Rose in the passenger seat of my car, tears streaming down her face. Saying to me she was pregnant. Both of us just kids. I was terrified and yet I knew what I had to do. I had to step up for her because she was everything to me, had been since I was fifteen. I knew I was going to spend my life with her. If she was having my baby, I would be there.

Behind this terror, there is no sureness. It's just fear. I draw away from her and stumble through my thoughts before I ask, limply, "Mine?"

"Yes."

I lean on my desk to brace myself. "But we just—last night, that's not enough time—"

"Not last night, Ash," Rye says with more patience than I deserve. "That wasn't the first time we... "

My mind flashes to the night a month and a half ago up at my house in Wilmette. Where we were secluded, away from the world, able to enjoy ourselves without threat, able to face the attraction we had been pushing down, which we probably had only been able to resist because we had never been truly, truly alone.

Why did we act so foolishly? No condom, no anything. I thought for sure she would have taken care of it. For sure she was... on something. "So... what do you want to do?"

Rye looks smaller than she's ever been. She's not objectively small. Smaller than me, but I'm taller than most. But now she shrinks away from me. This is not the reaction she probably wanted. I can't give her anything more.

"I can pay for you to get it taken care of. If that's what you want," I say with a swallow. It's not what I want. Not at all. Through all my fears, there is a warm feeling growing in the pit of my stomach. *We are bound.* In the most important, most beautiful way. I won't have her throw her life away for this baby. But I'd be lying if I didn't feel a primal pull toward her keeping it.

"No, I don't want to get rid of it. I want to keep it," Rye replies, her face screwed together to keep from crying. She drops one of her hands to her flat stomach which I can already picture growing, swelling with life. She'll look beautiful. She'll be a great mother.

Rye stares at me expectantly, waiting for me to say something. I have nothing. I don't deserve her. I don't deserve another chance with someone. After the way Rose died...

I don't deserve another chance at love. Not at all.

"Do you want to see?"

I look up to find Rye extending a blurry black and white ultrasound image toward me. It's too early to really tell it's a baby, but I've been here before and I know what to look for.

Fuck, this is real.

I take the image and cover my mouth. Tears are rushing into my eyes. I can't do this. *I can't do this.*

"I know it's inconvenient. I'm sorry I didn't... "

"Don't apologize, Rye." I stare a moment longer. In only weeks, the ultrasound will become more detailed, the fetus will develop into something resembling a baby, and Rye will grow and I'll... "I have a meeting to get to," I say, returning the image to her.

Rye's eyes widen, her fingers barely able to hold onto the image. She has no more words.

And neither do I. I push myself up from the desk and leave the office quickly, making sure she doesn't notice how badly I'm shaking. I go to my secretary immediately: "Cancel my day."

She starts to balk, to ask why, but I keep walking. I'm going home.

I wasn't strong enough to resist. And now I've ruined her life because of it.

I'm a monster.

Chapter 17

Rye

That couldn't have gone worse. Well, maybe if he had gotten angry. Thrown something. Maybe if there had been a cataclysmic event. Then it could have been worse.

But that went even worse than I expected.

I have to admit that I hoped upon hope that upon hearing the news Ash would embrace me, adamantly want to make this work between us. That he'd kiss me. He'd love me. Our baby...

How can I feel so low and so high at once? Because despite his rejection, I still am so committed to the child inside me, the one still fragile and delicate who needs me.

Someone needs me. I have to remember that. After months if not years of feeling extraneous in most people's lives, I have someone I need to show up for.

My baby. *My* baby. Not Ash's. That much is clear.

I return home; neither my dad nor Giselle are home, thank God. I'm sure he invited her to take my place at the lunch reservation. That's just as well. I go shut myself up in my room and lay in bed. How the fuck will I tell them?

There's no way I can tell them before the wedding. I can't add that to the stress of the day. I think I'll wait as long as I can. Get enough distance. That way I can pass it off as some one-night stand.

After crying for God knows how long and getting trapped in a cycle of thoughts, I pick up my phone and call Dara.

"Rye! I haven't heard from you in weeks, what's up?" Dara answers in her spirited, sweet way.

I immediately burst into tears. Her voice feels so safe, reminds me of all the time we spent wrapped in blankets on my couch watching shitty romcoms.

"Oh no, no, no, honey. What's going on? Is the wedding planning getting too stressful?"

"No, Dara, I've done something awful. Just awful."

She laughs, "I'm sure not. Lay it on me."

"I'm pregnant."

Dara gasps. "Oh my god! Well, that's not bad in and of itself. You have options. Who is the dad?"

I take a deep breath. "Ash."

The line goes silent. "Ash?" she finally says. "Like *the* Ash? The no-one-will-ever-compare-to-my-childhood-crush-so-I-may-as-well-not-date Ash???"

I don't reply. There's no other Ash.

Then Dara squeals so loud I have to pull the phone away from my ear. This should be, for all intents and purposes, an amazing thing. "I knew it! I knew you were hiding something! A big something! A big fucking something! This is so EXCITING!"

"It's not a *good* thing, Dara."

"Why? It's a great thing. Ashton Hawthorn is your baby daddy. What could be—oh, God," her joy halts and her voice gets cold, "Does your dad know?"

I sigh and sprawl out on my bed. "Let me explain everything."

So, I do. From day one to *now*. How it all came to pass that Ash and I became physically and, I guess, emotionally entangled. I explain our first encounter, the distance we enforced afterward, the phone calls (God, the phone calls), culminating with us fucking in my childhood bathroom and then this morning. When I found out I'm pregnant.

"Well, that's a lot," Dara says, totally enthralled.

"I know... "

"So, what are you going to do?"

I bury my face in my pillow. "I have no idea. I don't think I can tell anyone before the wedding. I think I just need to, I don't know. Lay low. And then I have to leave Chicago."

"But you just got there! You were so excited to get back."

I shake my head. "It's all different now. I won't be able to be here and have my baby and... Dara, Ash is my dad's best friend. I won't be able to get away from him."

"Well, your dad wouldn't be his best friend if he knew what he did to you."

I sit up and reply vehemently, "He didn't *do* anything to me. I was there too."

"I know, Rye."

"I was there. I chose it too," I trail off and then look out the window. The golden twilight is settling in the sky.

Dara hesitates. "I'm just saying, your dad is always going to choose you. Always."

That brings tears to my eyes. "I don't want him to choose me. I just wish this had never happened."

"Aww... " she coos over the phone. "Rye, honey, you don't wish that. You're having a baby."

I wipe away the tears running down my face quickly.

"I don't think that's something to wish never happened if you really want it. And it sounds like you do."

I smile through the pain. She's right. I made the decision as soon as I saw the ultrasound. I might not have my shit together, but I have all the love in the world to give a baby. I think about if my mother were here. I would have told her immediately. She would have come with me to the appointment. She would have told me that I know exactly what's right in my gut. She would have counted down from three and told me to make a split-second decision.

I would have said yes. Yes, I want the baby.

That's my answer.

Dara and I talk a bit longer and come up with a game plan. Right after the wedding, I'm going back to Madison. I can move in with Dara, get my bearings again. She says she can probably get me a job at the bakery she works at for the time being. I've got contacts still up that way. It might not be opening my own flower shop, but I'm sure I could find something. Anything.

I've got a baby to take care of.

Later, Giselle comes to my door. "Rye, honey. It's dinner."

"I'm not hungry tonight."

"Will you come down just to say hi? I haven't seen you all day."

I hold my breath and go to open the door.

Giselle stands there with a smile, but there's a bend to her brow. I can tell she's worried. Even though she's not my mom, she knows when something is up with me. I'm going to have to be a really good actor the next month and a half until I'm able to get out of town.

"You okay?" she asks. "You look like you've been crying."

It is unfortunate that I am a very bad actor. A bad liar. But this is not any normal circumstance. This is the difference between ruining the wedding and saving it. I won't ruin their wedding. Not when they deserve their day to be perfect.

"I'm just missing my mom," I say. It's not a lie. Not entirely. I wish she was here. I wish my mom was here to watch me become a mom myself.

"Oh, sweetheart... " Giselle says softly. "You want a hug."

I nod, but as soon as she embraces me, my heart starts thumping. What if she can feel the change in my body I can't yet see?

"I know how hard it can feel to not have that person around," she whispers in my ear. "You never have to feel scared about talking to me about her, though."

"I know," I say and slip my arms around her tightly. Probably the last meaningful hug we can have before my waist starts growing. Fuck, the dress for the wedding. I'm going to have to get that altered.

As we stand there, I make a quick mental to do list of how I'm going to have to hide this. First on the list, the dress.

Second on the list, never, ever speaking to Ashton Hawthorn again.

That one will be easy.

Chapter 18

Ash

I stare at Piper as she tumbles across the lawn, chasing skeins of bubbles that are floating through the air. Her feet are covered in dirt, her little yellow dress stained with grass, and she wears the biggest smile she can, her burbling giggle punctuating the quiet evening.

I cherish these moments I have with her. She's the light of my life. So much of Jarred in her, which means there's so much of *Rose* in her. From her light brown hair flecked with gold to full apples of her cheeks. When she smiles, I see my wife so clearly. Rose would have loved Piper. I wish she had been alive to meet her.

In a perverse way, I wish she was alive to meet *my* newest arrival. Although I'm not sure I can even claim that after the way I reacted to the news.

I've been trapped in a cycle of shame since Rye told me that she's pregnant. My reaction was fucking cowardly. Pitiful. That's not how a man should react to that sort of news. Especially not one of my age.

I couldn't stop thinking about Rose at first. I had just

gotten over the idea of being with another woman being a betrayal and now I was ostensibly starting a family with her.

No matter how much I thought about it though, I couldn't imagine Rose being mad. If she somehow apparated before me in this very moment, I couldn't imagine her being hurt or furious. I can only imagine her smile. I think that's what I've missed all along. Rose wouldn't have wanted me to be purposefully pulling myself away from love because of her. She'd want me to run toward it.

However, with how things have shaken out, if she apparated before me, I'm sure she'd call me an idiot. Lovingly, but still. An idiot.

Two weeks. I've known for two weeks that Rye is going to have my baby. And that's all I know. I haven't heard from her, haven't been able to speak to her.

I've tried to reach out to her. I've texted. I've called. I've sent emails. All of them unanswered.

I turn my phone over in my hand and open it up to our text conversation once more. It's pathetic, the paragraphs I've sent her. All detailing how sorry I am, how much I want to be a part of her life, how desperate I am for a second chance. At the very least, I want to be able to support her. Support my child. After all, it's my fault she's in this position. Sure, it takes two to tango, but I'm older, I'm wiser, and I have so much more power than she does without even trying. I have money and resources, I don't have to bear any physical brunt of bringing a child into the world, and she...

I wonder what her plan is. All of my communications with her father have been normal since I've found the news, even though I've definitely distanced myself. If he knew, I'm sure he would have immediately confronted me about it. Will she lie about who the father is?

That breaks my heart. On one hand, that she would feel

like she has to lie. On the other, that no one would know that *my child is mine.*

I start to type out a message against every kernel of rationality.

> Please let me show up for you. Please let me show you what kind of man I really am.

Send.

The text doesn't say it's delivered. She probably has my number blocked now. She's carrying my baby and she has my phone number blocked. If that isn't some sort of terrible karma, I don't know what is.

"Grampa!"

I look up to find Piper standing in front of me with her hands on her hips, pouting. "Yes, Pipes."

"You're not *watching* and now the bubble machine is out of bubbles," she says sadly, gesturing to the tiny plastic machine that's lamely sputtering with no bubbles in sight.

I tuck my phone back in my pocket and smile at her. Piper needs me, even if it's just to witness her. I can do that. "I'm sorry, baby girl. Let's fix that right now."

I pour more bubbles in the machine, Piper leaning on my leg the whole while. It bursts to life with bubbles again and she starts to frolic freely again. "Watch me pop the bubbles, Grampa!"

No more distractions. If I can't access Rye, can't prove to her what kind of man I am, then I have to show up in my own life for fuck's sake. "Not if I pop them first!"

The two of us clumsily dance around the yard trying to pop every bubble we can. I put on a show of being completely hapless at it so Piper gets to pop more. I try to stay focused on her, but I can't help thinking about this missed opportunity.

If I hadn't been such an ass to Rye, I'd be looking at a future full of lots more moments of childlike wonder. With my own child. Another one after all these years.

Since it's looking more and more as if it's not on the cards for me, I have to soak up all the time with Piper I can.

* * *

A little while later, Piper and I head inside, her balanced on my hips, head resting on my shoulder sleepily. My sons are posted up around the kitchen, tearing into takeout bags. Tonight, it's like four men and a baby, plus June. Rowan and Trevor are on a vacation together in Glacier National Park. Oliver's been antsy. He hasn't heard from either of them in a few days because the cell reception is so bad and they're spending most of their time hiking. It's hard when you're always the third wheel. I've been there. But I understand that he must also be worried sick.

These weekly dinners always come at a good time. Someone always needs a shoulder to lean on.

"Dinnertime, Pipes," Jarred says excitedly as we enter the kitchen.

Piper wriggles in my arms, reaching out for her dad. The only better feeling than having her in my arms is seeing how much she loves him.

"You definitely need a bath later, yikes," Jarred says as he takes Piper from me. He smells her dramatically and makes a face. "Stinky... "

She laughs. "I'm not stinky, Daddy. You're stinky!"

"Yes, and I'll take a bath later *too*."

Piper pouts.

"Oh come on, Piper," June says. "Baths are fun!"

The little girl frowns.

"Lots of bubbles... rubber ducks... splashing Daddy while he isn't looking," June lists, adding the last part under her breath, just for Piper.

"I heard that!" Jarred cries out.

Piper bounces excitedly. "Okay, I'll take a bath later."

I chuckle. "June always knows what to say."

June grins, teeth glimmering. "I've been around the block."

"Well, it was Oliver's night to choose," Keifer says with an eyeroll.

"Burgers!" Oliver announces excitedly, holding up a grease splotched, brown bag.

I groan. "Your taste, Oliver, is... "

"What's wrong with a burger?" he asks, grabbing a fry out of the bag and snarfing it down.

"Ask my arteries," I say. "Come on, let's eat."

We gather around the kitchen island on stools, Piper sitting at the head like the queen she is, even if she needs a booster seat.

It's a normal night for all intents and purposes, save the anxieties playing over and over in the back of my head. I'm barely able to entertain the conversation being had. Couldn't tell you what they're even talking about. These guys could talk each other's ears out about anything. They don't need my help propelling a conversation forward.

Looking at them, I realize. this is my family. My children, June, who is basically the daughter I never had. Piper, my grandchild. And yet, I keep imagining another place at the table. What would this dinner look like in a year if Rye gave me a chance to explain myself? What if she was mine? I could imagine her sitting beside me, baby wrapped in a sling at her chest. We'd both be tired, but it'd feel so nice to be there all together.

Wow, that's a nice picture. More than that. It feels good.

I glance around the table. Everyone is pretty much finished, most of the plates completely clean. Piper is getting squirmy. I've barely touched my food. My mind is far from here.

"Can I be done, Daddy?" Piper asks, kicking her feet.

"Sure, but we're getting right into bath," Jarred says, taking a final sip of his soda.

She whines, "I don't want to get a bath."

"Time for that bath, Pipes," he says, touching a knuckle to her chin.

Piper recoils from his touch. She's exhausted, teetering on the precipice of a tantrum. "I don't want to take a bath. I want to watch *cartoons*."

"My magic only goes so far," June laments.

Jarred does his best to smooth out Piper's distress. "Piper, honey, I'm sorry, but—"

"Go let her watch her show," I say abruptly.

Jarred glares at me. I'm not usually one to undercut his parenting, but when I do, it makes him edgy. "Dad, she's—"

"I need to talk with you three. Just let her watch her show. I'll give her a bath after," I say in a low voice.

The boys exchange glances with each other. I'm not usually this serious at our Sunday dinners.

"Thank you, Grampa!" Piper announces, clapping her hands together excitedly.

Jarred purses his lips aggravatedly and helps her down from the stool. I'll have to make good with him later.

"June, would you go with her?" I ask.

She's already caught on, clearing her plate and heading out the door. "Of course."

Piper scrambles after June, squawking excitedly. We all

wait until we hear the television turn on in the other room before anyone dares to speak.

"Is everything okay, Dad?" Oliver asks, polishing off the fries left on Piper's plate.

I chew on the inside of my lip; I scan their faces. All of them have hints of Rose, just like Piper. Jarred's got the blue of her eyes, Oliver the line of her nose, and Keifer the shape of her lips. If I truly believe that I have not betrayed Rose, I have to reconcile with the fact I may have betrayed the extensions of her still left on Earth.

They are owed my honesty.

"I need to talk to you about something."

"Are you okay? Like, are you healthy?" Oliver asks.

"I'm fine. It's not my health."

"Oh, thank god," Jarred says softly.

They collectively breathe a sigh of relief. I'm not that old, am I?

"So, what's going on?" Keifer asks. He's twisting his napkin through his fingers tensely.

"It's hard to say," I begin. "Because... well, you know how much your mother means to me. To all of us."

Oliver's eyes widen. "I knew it! You're seeing someone! Didn't I tell you guys?"

I freeze.

"You owe me twenty bucks," Oliver continues, punching Keifer playfully on the arm.

"Hold on, Dad hasn't *confirmed* yet, you've just assumed," Keifer retorts and then turns his gaze to me.

I'm not sure where to start. "I'm... what?"

"You've been acting funny lately," Jarred explains with a nonchalant shrug. "Oliver thought you might be seeing someone and too nervous to tell us."

Well, that sort of hits the nail on the head. "Um... well, yes. You're right. In some respects."

Oliver celebrates boisterously and shakes Keifer's shoulders. "You owe me twenty bucks!!!"

"Okay, okay, relax! Careful!" Keifer pushes Oliver off of him. "Congratulations, Dad."

Jarred smiles boldly, "It's about time!"

"You all... aren't upset with me?" I ask, my voice barely audible. I have never in all these years imagined this conversation would go over well.

"Why would we be?" Oliver scoffs. "You're a catch. I'm shocked it's taken this long."

His brothers nod in agreement.

"Well, um, there's a little more than that," I say, swallowing. "She's... she's pregnant."

The table goes silent and for a moment I think I'm about to be inundated with vitriolic jabs of "How could you?" and "What's wrong with you?" But instead, from the silence, comes even more excitement. I can't make heads or tails what the boys are saying, they're all so... thrilled. Jarred pats me on the back, Keifer beams, and Oliver enthusiastically launches himself toward the wine fridge to retrieve a bottle of champagne.

"Moving fast," Keifer chuckles.

"In classic Ashton Hawthorn fashion," Jarred says with a glint in his eye.

"Now, who is the lucky gal and when do we meet her?" Oliver chimes in.

My stomach drops. I feel faint. No, I feel like I'm going to vomit. Maybe both. "You already know her. "

Jarred and Keifer look at each other, no doubt trying to tabulate who it could possibly be. There aren't many viable options. "Who, Dad?" Jarred asks.

I pause. The only sound in the room the squeak of Oliver working the cork out of the bottle of champagne. I lick my lips, try to take a breath, but my heart is thumping so fast I may as well be running a marathon. "Rye Linden."

The champagne pops, but the room has completely deflated.

My boys stare at me as if I've started speaking a different language, mouths hanging open, eyes wide.

"Rye... Linden," Keifer repeats.

"Rye Linden as in Clay Linden... " Jarred processes aloud, his brow furrowing in horror.

"You mean... " Keifer's voice raises in pitch.

"You slept with Clay's daughter?!" Oliver cries out sharply, his hand wringing the neck of the champagne bottle.

I tuck my lips into my mouth, unwilling to confirm or deny what they've pretty well figured out.

"No wonder things were so weird when we went to the wedding venue, because you two were... " Oliver starts to pace back and forth. "Oh my god. How did this happen?"

"*Don't* answer that," Keifer says, cinching his eyes shut.

My eldest leans toward me. "She's my age, Dad."

"I know, I... let me explain how it happened."

I tell them the story with as few sordid details as I can. How it was platonic at first, but by spending so much time together, we connected. How both of us knew loss and spoke about it openly. How I hadn't felt this way about a woman in years. And how I've pushed her away.

"It felt inevitable," I say, finally having explained all the details I could possibly share. "And I've totally screwed everything up."

"Does Clay know?" Oliver asks.

"No. At least I haven't told him."

Jarred runs a hand over his face. "Oh god."

"I know. It's messy. It's... very messy." I look at each of them as steadily as I can. "You know me, I don't just do things for the sake of doing them. The last thing I wanted to do was hurt anyone. I understand if you're angry with me or—"

"Are you kidding?" Keifer interrupts. "I'm not going to pretend like it's not weird. But you love her, don't you?"

My blood runs cold. I haven't said that out loud, but I've felt it. "I want an opportunity to love her the way she deserves. She's an amazing woman. I know it's so... " I trail off and my jaw trembles. Tears well into my eyes.

"Oh, Dad... " Jarred tuts.

"I'm sorry," I say, covering my eyes. I don't want to cry. I'm not the victim. But I can't help it. I've been strong for so many years, resisted every impulse I've had to moving on after Rose's death, blamed myself for so long...

I'm giving up.

I love that girl. I love Rye Linden.

My sons crowd around me, wrapping me in their arms. I reach for them as best I can, remembering when each of them was small enough to fit in just the crook of my arm. And now here they are, comforting me.

"Dad, don't worry," Oliver says, rubbing my back. "You're getting her back."

"We'll make sure of it," Keifer adds.

"Grampa's sad?"

We all turn toward the door where Piper stands, holding her favorite stuffed bunny. A quizzical look on her face. June peeks around the doorframe too. "Sorry... I tried to stop her."

I can tell by the look on June's face that she overheard enough to gather the details. "It's okay, June."

Jarred goes to her and scoops her off the ground. "Yeah, honey. Why don't you comfort him?"

All my sadness dissipates as Jarred brings her to me, Piper's face full of naïve concern. She reaches around my neck and pulls herself onto my lap and close as she can be. "What's wrong?" Her dainty voice is so tender, I almost weep more.

"I've hurt someone pretty badly, Pipes."

She frowns. "Did you mean to?"

"Well, not really," I say through half a laugh. "But I did. And now they're really upset with me."

"Say you're sorry, then!" she replies as if it's the easiest thing in the world. She wraps her bitty hands around my face, pushing on my cheeks. "And then give them a kiss!"

We all laugh.

"You have no idea how much he'd like that, Pipes," Oliver says wryly.

"Shut up, man. You're gross," Keifer spars back.

Keifer and Oliver start to go at each other and Jarred attempts to peace keep, leaving me and Piper alone.

She plants a kiss right on my forehead. "Like that."

"I'll keep that in mind," I tell her and pull her tighter in my arms.

Chapter 19

Rye

"I don't think I'm very good at this."

I look over at Giselle's canvas and have to hold in a snort. What is supposed to be a man's bare chest with a tie loosened around his neck looks more like a topographical map of puffy mountains and a messy river delta. "I think it's good."

She glares at me. "You're lying." Then, she reaches for her nearly drained wine glass and takes the final sip. "Okay, we're going abstract. I need more wine."

We've gone for a more unconventional bachelorette party than what you would see in the movies. No *Magic Mike* here. Just us girls doing one of those trendy painting classes where you get drunk while doing them.

"White or red?" I ask.

"Red."

I reach for one of the bottles on the table and shake it to see if it sloshes. Then, I pour her a glass.

"Rye. Have a glass. Please. I'm begging you," Giselle moans, clutching my arm.

"Can't. Designated driver," I say for the fiftieth time of the night.

"One glass and you'll be fine to drive!" she says, snatching the bottle from me. "Can we get another glass?" she calls out to the instructor who has been circling the table and complimenting our work.

I blanche. "I'm really fine." I obviously haven't told her the real reason I'm not drinking. Drinking for two probably doesn't have the same ring it did back in the fifties.

"No, you have to start drinking," Celia slurs in my ear. "Your painting is much too nice."

I look at my version of the bare-chested man and sigh. Sure, I guess it resembles the example set by the instructor pretty closely, but I know that I'm going to throw this thing right in the trash when I'm done with it.

I hate that I'm thinking about Ash. This faceless, bare-chested painting has my brain mushy. It doesn't even look like his chest. Ash is covered in hair and while he's definitely toned, he's not ripped to shreds like this guy.

It's been difficult to push him away, especially since he's always reaching out. I finally had to block his phone number. At least then I only have to worry about him popping into my email inbox. I can't cut off communication completely. After all, there are still lots of last-minute details we need to take care of so the wedding goes off without a hitch. I'm good about communicating about the wedding. It's just business, there's no need to get emotional.

It's when *he* tries to go beyond it that I get all out of sorts. I'm pregnant with his baby, it's not like I can just shut off my emotions. Not to mention all the hormones I'm already starting to feel kick into gear.

He had his chance. And he fucked it up royally when he abandoned me in his office. It doesn't matter how many sweet messages he tries to send with promises of working things out, of taking care of me and our baby, of *trying to make things right.* There's nothing he can do to make things right when they're already so wrong. Wrong from the very beginning.

Just tonight, before Giselle and I left the house for the party, I received an email from him: *Be safe tonight.*

I've been running the message over and over in my head. What the hell does that mean? It's not like we're going out bar hopping. In fact, it's the guys who need to "be safe" because they're going to a club. Giselle thought it was awfully funny, the thought of my dad and all his friends at a fancy club with bottle service and the works. Dad didn't seem that interested, but with the party planning left to the groomsmen, that's the party he's getting.

Be safe. I'm just sitting with some girls painting. All I can imagine is that he's telling me not to drink which I resent completely. As if he has any right to be in my business after everything he's put me through.

Put *us* through. Me and *my* baby.

The instructor sets a glass out beside my canvas and Giselle thanks her while pouring me the fullest glass of wine I've ever seen.

"Giselle, really—"

I am met with jeers from the bridal party. Celia grabs the wine glass off the table and sticks it right in my hand. "Drink! Aren't you young? You won't even get a hangover?"

I swallow. I can get away with one sip, right? I don't *want* it, but if I have to keep up appearances, I might have to. I bring the glass toward my lips, but when the scent of red wine hits my nose, my stomach flips. I recoil. Nausea settles in the pit of my throat.

What they don't tell you about "morning sickness" is

that it's actually "all the time sickness". Plus, I've been extremely sensitive to smells since finding out I'm pregnant. Onions, patchouli, *red wine*.

I push my chair out from the table and shove my glass into Giselle's hand. The wine sloshes over the sides, but I don't care. "I need a bathroom." My stomach heaves upward and I hold back a gag.

The instructor looks at me with big, worried eyes and gestures to a short corridor. I rush as fast as I can, gripping at any doorknob I can find, until I stumble into a warmly lit, tiny bathroom where there's barely enough room for me to bend over the toilet.

I gag, sputter, and then all the contents of my guts splatter into the toilet. *Jesus fucking Christ.*

The first couple weeks were fine, but it's just getting worse. It's getting harder to hide. I'm starting to notice that my belly is starting to tense as well, even though there's not a bump yet. There's not much time before I can't hide it anymore.

Thank God we're one week away from the wedding. I've made all the arrangements to get back to Madison the very next day. Then I don't have to worry about anyone's suspicions. When I told Dad and Giselle, they were definitely disappointed to hear I'd be leaving. My dad pushed back quite a bit, but Giselle made him back down. "If she knows what's right for her, we have to trust her."

I don't know what's right for me. But it's nice to know people believe I do.

"Rye?"

I turn to find Giselle in the doorway. Fuck, I forgot to lock it.

"Oh, sweetie... I'm sorry," she says softly. "I didn't mean to—"

"It's okay," I say. "It's f—" I'm hit with another wave of nausea and clutch my belly before vomiting again.

Giselle pulls my hair away from my face and rubs my back softly.

"You should go have fun, it's your bachelorette party. You shouldn't—"

"Shhh... "

I gag once more, spit into the toilet, and then am able to catch my breath. My eyes are totally bleary with tears. Everything burns.

"I didn't know you weren't feeling well. You didn't have to come out if you weren't—"

"Giselle, I'm fine. Really," I say.

Our eyes meet. I suck in my lower lip. Giselle's brown eyes are hardened in mine.

"Rye. You know I can tell when you're lying."

I hold my breath. Is she saying what I think she's saying? Does she know? Can she tell? Is it obvious?

"Is there something you need to tell me?"

I try to laugh. "No, no, what would I need to... "

"You haven't been drinking. You've been getting sick lately and not telling anyone."

I frown. I really thought I'd been getting away with sneaking into the bathroom early in the mornings.

"Rye, what's going on?" she says, leaning close to me. "You can tell me. I promise, I won't say anything if it's—'"

"I just haven't been feeling well," I cut her off. "I think I'm just nervous about the wedding. All the planning. I'm just getting nervous, I guess."

The corners of Giselle's eyes tighten and she looks away. "Okay." She knows I'm lying. She knows what's going on. She's not an idiot. She knows the signs. Giselle grabs a piece of toilet paper and starts to dab at my under eyes where my mascara has started to run. "Let's clean you up."

We sit on the floor of this tiny bathroom, her getting me cleaned up, me holding onto this lie until I can't anymore. I can tell she's hurt. And I wish I could go back. Perhaps I should have told her from the start. Maybe I could have had her with me in this from the very beginning.

It's too late now.

"Just know that I'm always here for you, honey. Okay?" she says, cupping my cheek.

I nod. "Thanks, Elle."

"Now, if you want to go home and rest—"

I laugh. "No way, I'm not ditching your bachelorette party just because I got a little sick." I get to my feet and dust off my dress. "I'll be fine."

"Okay, only if you're sure," she says and puts her hand delicately on my lower back. Her fingers curl to my waist the slightest bit. She's measuring, thinking, wondering if she's crazy.

I'll let her believe she is. We'll both pretend we don't know what's happening. Until we no longer can.

Chapter 20

Ash

I should have made up an excuse not to be here tonight. I left clubbing behind when I... well, I've never liked clubs. I've only ever been to them when I'm trying to entertain clients. Some of those older businessmen love the flash and flair of being taken out somewhere they simply do not belong and to have beautiful girls serve them.

This wouldn't have been my choice. But I left the planning to Clay's college buddies and they... lack finesse, to put it nicely.

Clay is fucking wasted. It's honestly hilarious the way he's tripping over himself and burbling nonsense. I've been tasked with keeping an eye on him, which I'm more than happy to do.

Because after tonight, I don't know the next time my friend will want to hang out with me. Don't know if he'll ever want to again. I'm resigned to the fact that the truth is going to come out eventually. I certainly won't be the one to tell him. I think that'd be an insult to Rye. I thought about it, in fact, when talking over how to win Rye back with my sons, they suggested it might be a good idea for me to take ownership of the situation and maybe that would prove to her that I wasn't a coward.

Something about that doesn't sit right with me, though. If either of us has to lose Clay, it should be me.

Clay leans over and grabs me by the shoulder, loudly shouting in my ear, "You look *bummed.*"

"I look bummed?" I say with a wry smile.

"Yeah. You look pissed. Like you don't want to be here."

I grimace. "I do?"

Clay nods excessively and sips through a cocktail straw from a drink I'm not sure was his to begin with.

"I'm sorry. I'm just thinking. Wedding stuff, you know?"

"I should be thinking about wedding stuff! Not you!" Clay cries out, smacking me on the arm. He catches the attention of our cocktail waitress, a cute girl with long legs and bleach blonde hair with a voice low and sweet like a black cherry. "He needs a drink."

The girl leans toward me and I can see straight down her bustier top between her breasts. She smiles at me like she could eat me. "What do you want, honey?"

"Scotch. On the rocks," I say, unable to think of anything else.

"What kind of scotch?"

I sigh. "Surprise me."

She smirks. "I can do that." Then she struts off.

Clay looks at me with wide eyes; even in the flashing lights of the club, I can tell they're just as blue as Rye's. I can't help but wonder if our baby will have the same eyes. I want to run away and bury my head in the sand. "She likes you," he says with a cocked grin.

"Maybe," I say, casting my eyes down.

"Maybe? Maybe??? You're crazy," he says, clapping me on the back. "You've got to get back out there, Ash. You're...

you're... " Clay searches for the right word. "*Hot,* as the girls would say."

I laugh. "Is that what girls say?"

"Listen, I'm trying to tell you in an objective way that you're an attractive man."

Our waitress returns with my scotch centered on a black tray. "Surprise for you, sir," she says, holding the tray down to my eye level.

"Thank you."

"Don't mention it."

She struts off again.

"That was your moment! That was your moment and you missed it."

I sip the scotch. It's smoky and sharp at once. "First of all," I say through the bitterness. "She's working. She doesn't need any more guys hitting on her than already are."

"Man, see, that's what I've always loved about you," Clay says. "You're respectful. You know how to treat women. I hope Rye can find someone like you."

I hope he doesn't notice how my eyes bug out at the sound of that and carry on as if what he said hasn't just slain me. "And *second of all,* you lucked out. Not everyone can find their Giselle."

"No, that's true," Clay says, looking off into the distance with dreamy eyes. "She's going to marry me. *Me.* Can you believe it?"

I smile. "What you don't have in looks, you make up for with heart. Of course, I can believe it."

He snickers. "I hate you." He slinks his arm around my shoulder. "You have no idea how much all this wedding stuff has meant to me, Clay. That you've helped Rye so much... that you've taken so much time." Clay is getting choked up. Dear god. I can't do this. "Means a lot to me."

"Don't mention it," I say in a distant way. Conversation over.

Clay's college buddies, Ted and Fred (I wish I was making this up) barrel over. They are drenched in sweat. They've been dancing for the past hour. They both collapse on the long soft bench that encircles our table and wriggle up to Clay, palling around.

I'm able to sneak away without anyone noticing. I just need a breath of fresh air. I'd like nothing more than to go home, but if I have to stick out the rest of the night, then I will.

I shimmy through the crowds until I'm able to make it onto the balcony that overlooks the city. There are groups of people scattered about, but there's a perfect opening for me to sidle on up to the railing and just take a moment to myself.

I pull my phone out of my pocket, praying as I've prayed every time I look at my phone over the past few weeks that there will be a message from Rye, but no such luck. I purse my lips.

Something Jarred said to me echoes in my head: "Keep trying." Such a simple statement. And yet, I can't help but repeat it to myself. Keep trying, keep trying, keep trying.

I open up the Notes app on my phone and start typing out my thoughts.

I want to be there for you.

Keifer told me, "Be specific." I have to remember that too.

I want to be there to hold your hair when you're sick.

And Oliver said, "Tell the truth."

I want to be there to watch you grow. I want to be a part of this with you.

"You didn't like the drink, huh?"

I shut off my phone and tuck it away like it's a government secret and turn to find the waitress standing beside me, her hand on her hip. Man, she's tall. She comes up past my shoulder. "No, no, it was great," I say. "I just left it to catch my breath for a second."

She looks over her shoulder at our table. "You having a good night?"

"Yeah. Yeah."

She smiles. "Could be better, I take it."

"Well. Yes. But this night isn't about me, you know how it is."

She nods, her blonde hair bouncing. "I do. I really do."

It feels like she's measuring me up. Maybe she's flirting with me. I don't know how I'll let her down easy. Don't know if I could. I'm so fucking lost. Maybe if she offered, I should just let her do whatever she wants to me. Perhaps that would help with letting Rye go the littlest bit. There are plenty of fish in the sea, right?

Instead, though, she points to my pocket and says, "You're thinking about someone."

I chuckle to myself. "Yeah."

"Not getting a reply?"

"Is it that obvious?"

She shrugs. "We've all been there, I think."

I nod and pull my phone out of my pocket again, checking for a text I know isn't there.

"Can I give you a piece of advice?"

"I'll take whatever I can get, at this point."

The waitress looks out at the skyline and then smiles sadly. "Don't send the text. Just enjoy yourself so future you doesn't regret spending your friend's bachelor party moping over a girl."

I laugh. If only she knew how complicated it actually was. And yet...

She's right. This is Clay's night. I'm here for him. And I need to show up for him. Even if it is the last time.

"Thanks," I say and turn off my phone. "You're totally right."

She sighs. "Wish I wasn't. Anyway. Have fun."

I do. I go back to the table. Have a couple more drinks until Clay is well and truly spent, leaning on my shoulder for support, burbling about God knows what. Something about Giselle, something about Heather, something about Rye. All the women in his life. He's gushing, mushy, near tears over everything.

I take him home and leave the rest of the guys to enjoy themselves. When I pull up to the Linden household, the outside light is on and so is one light in one of the upstairs windows. I wonder if it's Rye's room.

I get Clay up the stairs and Giselle meets us, taking his limp, stumbling form in her arms and supporting him with all the strength she can muster. They smile at each other, so deeply in love, it doesn't matter how drunk or silly one of them is.

"Thanks, Ash," Giselle says to me before taking Clay inside.

I'm so close to Rye. I could force my way into the house, find her, demand she speak to me.

But not tonight. Not ever. Rye will be ready when she's ready. If she's ever ready.

It's the if that scares me.

I spend the night at the apartment, laying in my empty king-sized bed, thinking nonstop about Rye. Her beautiful ocean eyes, the dark skeins of her hair, the soft curve of her waist, the feeling of her lips on mine. Her bubbling laughs. The way she plays with her necklace when she's nervous.

I love her.

And I may have to learn how to live with her never loving me back.

* * *

Dinner is quiet. Too quiet. I swore everyone to secrecy.

"You all must be excited for the wedding," Rowan says bitterly.

"Ro..." Trevor runs her hand over her back.

"I'm just sad everyone is going except for us," she says sadly.

Trevor rubs her back. "Rowan, we don't know them really all that well."

"I know we don't know them, I just–" She crosses her arms over her chest. "I hate missing out. We'll all be at dinner next week and you all will have these stories. Like 'Oh my god, can you believe the DJ played that song?' or 'Oh my god, can you believe the father of the bride did *that*?' or–"

"Oh my god," Trevor says with a chuckle.

Rowan frowns. "I'm big enough to admit I'm jealous."

"You can go with me, Ro. I don't have a date," Oliver jokes before taking a sip of his beer.

"Trevor, you go with Oliver too. Then you three can be a throuple."

Piper's ears perk up at that moment. "What's a throuple?" You can always count on children to be aware at the exact moment you don't want them to be.

"Don't you worry about that. Eat your peas," Jarred says before shooting a glare at Keifer. "Do you mind?"

Keifer snorts.

"You guys are so immature sometimes, I swear," I say dryly.

The boys all look at me with various levels of pity; I wish I hadn't said anything at all. They've all been tiptoeing around me ever since they found out about Rye and me. June too, but less so. She's been good about ignoring that she heard anything at all.

"Man, you going to a wedding or a funeral, Mr. H? You look..." Trevor scrutinizes my face.

"Disturbed," Rowan finishes plainly.

"I wasn't gonna say disturbed," Trevor says to Rowan. "But now that you say it –"

"I'm fine," I say. "Thanks. But. I'm fine."

Trevor's eyes narrow. "Dower, maybe."

Oliver grabs his friend by the arm. "Hey, lay off it, man, will you?"

Trevor's blue eyes widen. "Sorry, I'm just–just worried about you, Mr. H. You've been a little different lately. Maybe we just missed it because of our trip or–"

"I'm just worried about the wedding. Want it to go well," I say, jaw tensing.

"Of course, it will! You've been working so hard on it. You and what's-her-name. It's like a type of bread, right?" Rowan goes on in her well-meaning, class clown way.

Ire burns inside me. It's not her fault. I know it isn't. She doesn't know. But that's the mother of my child she's talking about. Not some type of bread. "*Rye.*"

"Rye! Exactly. You and Rye have been working so hard on it."

I tense my knuckles under the table. I need to step away before I say something I regret. "I need some air."

I get up suddenly and walk out onto the terrace, all the

way down the path to the lake. I don't look back once. When I'm there, looking out at the spattered orange sky of Lake Michigan, I'm reminded of the first time out here with Rye. I can feel her here with me. Who would've thought some wine and the intoxication of a beautiful view would have gotten us here? I go to the edge of the seawall and sit down, dangling my legs over the edge. Water laps against the rocks below. So calm. So opposite how I feel inside.

"Hey."

I turn to find Jarred at the mouth of the path. He's got his hands in his pockets.

"I can leave you alone if you want, but–"

"No, no. Come sit."

Jarred sits beside me. "Oliver was going to come after you, but I thought it'd be best if I did it."

I glance at him. A soft breeze blows through the long locks of blonde hair, the ones I hated when he was a teen and now are so much a part of him I can't imagine him with hair any shorter.

"You know, I think I'm the only one who might understand. At least a little."

"Hm. Yeah. You're right."

We look out at the water in silence. My firstborn, the father of my only grandchild. The only father out of all the kids I spend my Sunday nights with. We can relate that way. And while I've been at it a lot longer than him, there's a camaraderie in sharing that type of identity.

"I'm scared," I say.

Jarred nods. "I know."

"I want to do it right."

"I know."

"I know you know."

I purse my lips tight together, furrowing my brow,

looking at the miles of water before us. "Why won't she let me?"

Jarred hesitates. "I don't know, Dad. All I know is that these things are a lot more complicated than we were led to believe as kids."

I laugh and gaze down at my hands in my lap. "I'm sorry if I made it look uncomplicated."

"Don't apologize, Dad. You've done great."

We exchange a smile.

"I don't want to speak for Rye. I don't know her really at all. But I'm sure that once the baby is born, she'll realize how important it is to have you in the baby's life. You're a good man, Dad."

His words of inspiration don't make me feel anything but sadness. "That's just the thing, Jare. I don't want to wait. I can't... it's too painful." I swallow. "I want her now."

Jarred is silent. Then he wraps his arm over my shoulder and whispers. "Then go fucking get her."

Chapter 21

Rye

I tug on the skirt of my dress to make it lay nicer around my hips. The champagne satin shows every imperfection, every shadow on my body. Most people wouldn't be caught dead with their Maid of honor wearing a remote shade of white, but Giselle thought the color would look beautiful with her bright orange gown.

"Like a mimosa," she had announced cheerfully when she settled on the color.

I adjust the cowl neck slightly and then tuck a loose curl behind my ear, staring into the mirror at myself. My hair is pulled back in an elaborate updo, a lily tucked into the roulade of hair.

I'm surprised by how beautiful I feel.

The rest of the bridal party has moved outside, excitedly waiting for the first look, but I've remained behind to get a moment alone with myself. It's a strange feeling that I can never *truly* be alone with myself anymore. At least for the next seven-ish months. I've got another passenger with me.

Dara says she can't imagine being in my shoes. "I think

I'd feel so lonely," she said to me on the phone the other night as I was informing her of all my flight information.

I don't feel lonely. How could I? I've got my baby.

I check the room once more out of paranoia before turning to the side to observe my profile. Miraculously, there's no sign of the pregnancy. In just the last few days, I've noticed the slightest curve starting to form in my belly, a curve only I could notice, especially since I've been watching it like a hawk. Just to be safe, I'm wearing some Spanx.

Sometimes, I get flashes of what I'll look like in seven months. Big, round, swollen. I don't know if I'll feel as confident as I do now. Maybe I'll wish I had someone by my side to share this with.

I have to face Ash today. For the first time since I told him the news. I'm terrified. But I know I have all the power. This is my dad's big day. He'd be a fool to spoil it or make a scene.

I will get through this. I'll see him and perhaps exchange a few polite words. The thing I'll have to worry about getting through is our dance; not sure why Giselle was so set on the extremely antiquated tradition of the best man and maid of honor dancing, but maybe that's a testament to the positive impression we've given everyone. Ash and I just work *so well* together.

Too well.

My eyes well up with tears. Fuck. I can't cry. The ceremony hasn't even started and I *know* I'm going to weep through that. I lean my head back to try and keep the tears in my eyes. *Deep breaths, Rye.*

The most painful part is how close I was to having the life I always dreamed of. Since I was just a girl, with delusions of grandeur about Ashton Hawthorn, my dad's handsome best friend. That this dream so nearly came true. That's the problem, isn't it? I brushed up against it, too close, *way* too close. And now I'm pregnant. Serves me right, I guess.

I shake off the tears and force a smile. "I'm fine, I'm fine." I'll be far away from Chicago come tomorrow morning. Then I can start my new life.

"Just you and me, Butterbean," I say to the baby, running my hand up and down my stomach. The nickname came from a can of beans Dad had out while he was making some sort of soup a week or so ago. I'd never even known butterbeans were a thing. And when I said it out loud, I just thought it suited my little bean so well. Butterbean. Baby Butterbean. Hopefully, I can keep my wits about me through this pregnancy, so I don't impulsively *actually* name the baby Butterbean.

I hear the doorknob jostle behind me and immediately draw my hand away from my stomach.

"Rye, you're going to miss it," Celia calls to me in an eager whisper.

I turn on my heel and rush out of the room. "Thanks for getting me."

Celia smiles. She's still wearing her thick, black-rimmed glasses which look funny when compared with how done up she is. "You look beautiful," she says to me and squeezes my waist.

I'm very grateful that leading up to today, Celia has really stepped up. I've done my part but getting the flowers together has taken all my time and energy. She's been really fantastic about letting me delegate to her.

We walk to the end of the hall and gather with the other bridesmaids who are all peering around the corner. I see my father and Giselle standing back-to-back. The photographer, a young woman named Lucy with one long braid down her back, is capturing every angle of the moment. She was Ash's choice. He liked her work, the way she edited colors, the angles she used.

"You ready?" the photographer asks them with a toothy grin.

Giselle reaches for my dad's hand. She looks beautiful. He's going to flip. She could have shown up in sweatpants and a dirty t shirt and he would have lost his mind, but seeing Giselle in her beautiful orange dress, her hair elaborately wrapped up, her lips bathed in a rosy, red color is going to kill him.

I haven't gotten a good look at my dad yet, but his salt and pepper hair is swept back in a smooth curl, mostly distracting from the spot on the back of his head where his hair is thinning. His suit is a beautiful dark blue which compliments her dress perfectly.

"Ready, baby?" she asks him.

Dad doesn't reply, just turns around, anticipation throttling through him like a kid about to be served an ice cream sundae. I don't think he gets a good look at her before he bursts into tears.

"I'm not going to cry," I say and start fanning my eyes.

The other bridesmaids pat my back and hold me tight. This is too much for me. When Mom was alive, I obviously knew my dad loved her. It was quite obvious, even if they weren't incredibly touchy or overtly affectionate. Even on their worst days, I knew they'd work it out. We were a perfect trio. A family. And when Mom died, Dad and I... I don't know if we were a dynamic duo. We always had our third person there to bring us together. The glue. My mom.

Seeing my dad fall in love and finding a future he didn't know was possible has been one of the greatest gifts of my life. It's not the same trio we had before. No one can ever replace my mother, but gosh, is it different. And I'm really fucking grateful for it.

Giselle and Dad embrace, share a delicate kiss. My dad wants more, but she waves him off. "My makeup, Clay!"

"You're so beautiful," he says in a trembling voice. He wraps her face in his hands and my heart breaks. My mind flashes to the person I wish I could share that kind of moment with. I avert my eyes and try to breathe through the thought of Ash seeing me in a wedding dress and having that same kind of reaction.

Dani, serving as the coordinator for the day, sidles up beside me and touches my arm. "Time to get the bouquets ready."

I take a deep breath. Time to do what I do best.

* * *

The bridal party congregates around me outside the ceremony hall. I can hear the wedding guests chattering inside. Everyone holds their bouquets out before them and I go down the line, one by one, perfecting the work I've already slaved over. I trim back filler, gently massage hydrangea blooms, and add small sprigs of myrtle.

When I get to Giselle, she pulls the bouquet back from me. "Giselle, please, let me just—"

"It's perfect the way it is. It's a Rye creation. I can't imagine anything more perfect," she says with a proud smile.

I look down at her bridal bouquet. It bustles and blooms with elegance and distinction. She's right. It's perfect. Needs no more anxious preening from me.

"I think someone wants to talk to you," she says with a nod past me.

My heart drops. My mind immediately goes to Ash, but when I turn, I see my dad. He's holding his boutonniere, a white anemone with a big, bold yellow center. "Help me put this on?" he asks me.

I nod bashfully.

Dad leads me away from the hubbub into a private part of the corridor and hands me the flower. I smooth out his lapel to prime it for the boutonniere. I have a million things I'd like to say, but I'm completely silent.

"Rye, honey?"

"Yeah, Daddy."

My dad takes a deep breath. "I still love your mom," he says. It is not an admission, but an explanation. "I miss her every day."

"I know. Me too," I say softly, pinning the flower to his jacket. I smile. It looks awfully nice, the white flower juxtaposed with yellow yarrow.

"I don't want you to ever feel like I've... moved on or I've—"

"Dad, I don't think that," I say and look into his eyes.

His smile curls to the side. "You're the best thing that's ever happened to me, Rye."

Again, the tears. "Dad, don't make me cry, the wedding hasn't even happened and—"

"Aw, baby, come here." He wraps his arms around me and holds me close. I bury my face in his shoulder; he's holding his only child and his only grandchild. He just doesn't know it yet. I hope one day he'll look back on this moment and see how special it truly was, even if I've made a huge mistake. "You're so much like her. Not just the way you look, but your heart. And as long as you're alive, I know she's not far. I just want you to know that."

I can't help but think about the child growing inside me. When I hold him or her, will I have the same gratitude for the indelible connection they give me to Ash? I'm afraid of how much I'll think about Ash for... well, the rest of my life. My child is inextricably linked to him, whether I want to admit it or not. When he or she is born, there will inevitably be parts of them that resemble their father.

"I love you, Rye."

I push those thoughts away and hold my dad tighter. "I love you, Daddy."

Nothing will spoil his day. Not a damn thing.

Chapter 22

Ash

I haven't stood in someone's wedding in a long time. And this one is the most important of all.

The ceremony hall looks incredible, the decorations pristine and perfect, exactly as Rye and I had arranged them.

It's impossible not to think about Rye today. For one, I'll get to see her again. After all this time. Finally. But also, we are ensconced in every detail. In the way the lights are hung, in the color of the floor runner, in the choice of chairs for the guests. We did that all together. Except for the flowers. I feel faint at the thought that Rye put together the boutonniere on my lapel. It lays right over my heart, right where I keep her.

I straighten up and hold my head higher, giving a look to my boys who are sitting in the back. They're all watching the door eagerly, waiting for Rye to come out.

Beside me, Clay stands with the steadiness of a windsock. He's sweating. I reach into the pocket of my trousers and hand him a handkerchief. "Here, buddy," I whisper.

"Thank you," he mutters and pats his forehead. "You came prepared."

"What's a best man for?" For having a handkerchief and giving a pep talk.

Not fucking the maid of honor who also happens to be the groom's daughter and getting her pregnant.

The bridesmaids and groomsmen walk down the aisle in pairs. My heart galumphs in my chest. The anticipation is killing me. This morning, I woke up and my first thought was Rye. All I wanted to know was if she was feeling alright.

This early in all of Rose's pregnancies, she was sick as a dog in the mornings. Thinking of Rye doing this alone makes me feel so helpless.

By the way Giselle and Clay have been treating me all morning, I know they don't know about the baby, or if they do, they sure as hell don't know it's mine.

Even though the music doesn't change and everyone in the crowd is waiting to see Giselle, the world stops when Rye comes into view. I feel like I might cry as if it's my own wedding when I see her. "Wow," I can' t help but whisper.

"She looks beautiful, doesn't she?" Clay asks with a proud smile.

What's a word more than beautiful? Rye's dress drapes over her body as if she's a Grecian statue, a goddess. Her hair is coiled back on top of her head, giving me a perfect view of her face. Her eyes, clear and confident as she looks down the aisle at her father.

Though she's not visibly pregnant, I can see the microscopic changes in her. I know her body so well. A slight fullness to her cheeks, heaviness in her breasts, wideness to her hips.

Rye glows. There's no better way to say it. And she's carrying my baby.

When she arrives at the altar, she greets her father with a kiss. For a split second, I wonder if he's about to pass her off to me, forgetting this isn't my wedding and there's no need for him to give her away.

I try to catch her eye for a brief moment, but she avoids my gaze completely, going to the spot parallel to mine with the other bridesmaids.

Then, the music changes, the guests all stand, and Giselle appears at the end of the aisle and that's when I come back to Earth and remember this isn't my wedding.

* * *

I'm glad I prepared for worst case scenario because that's how this is all going. Okay, to be fair, worst-case scenario would have been Rye having told Clay about everything and then Clay decided to square up on his wedding day.

Although that might have been better than this. Through everything, Rye has not looked at me. Not fucking once. Not while the wedding party was taking photos, not as we were waiting to enter the reception, and now, not during dinner either. We're even sitting across from each other at the head of the table, Giselle and Clay sitting at the very head on a loveseat just for them. She's managed to make the pears on her salad look incredibly interesting, the way she's staring at them. And of course, I'm not going to approach her. I'm not going to engage her in a conversation. She has to come to me.

I get a pang in my heart from time to time when I remember the baby. It's never far from my mind, but it still feels like I'm imagining it. she's still at a point she can pretend that it doesn't exist, so that's what I have to do too.

"I love the music, Ash," Giselle says to me with a smile.

I glance over at the band. DeFUNK is *really* bringing the DeFUNK. And it's just dinner. Who knows how it will be when the dance floor is pumping?

"I'm glad you like them. We were nervous it'd be too... funky," I say with a fleeting glance to Rye. Nothing. *Dammit.*

"Oh, I love it. It's memorable. And their costumes are ridiculous," Clay says excitedly with a burbling laugh. He's already had too much champagne. The nerves really got to him.

Giselle puts her hand on his wrist to ground him and he smiles at her dearly.

I look at the band again. That's the only thing I have going for me. Per tradition, the maid of honor and the best man are supposed to have a dance together after the bride and groom's first dance. I'm suddenly grateful that Giselle and Clay insisted on this tradition. They think it'll be a good way to break the ice and get people excited to get up and dance.

Rye will have to look at me then. Even if she doesn't say anything, I can say plenty.

Suddenly, the music stops and DJ announces, "Time for speeches from our wedding party. First, Mr. Ashton Hawthorn, best man."

I get up. I have my speech tucked into my breast pocket on a notecard, but I don't think I need it. It's nothing much. I'm not very good with sentimental words, but I did my best for Clay. It's already emblazoned on my mind. DJ hands me the microphone and I scan the crowd. "I'll make this short and sweet. Just like Clay."

The room erupts with laughter; Clay guffaws, "Everyone's short to you!"

I grin. Even Rye has cracked a small smile. And even though she won't look at me, I have her with me. The boutonniere on my chest, her creation, has been my totem this entire evening. "Anyway. Giselle, Clay is my best friend. We've been through tough times together. Really tough. And at times, it felt like we were the only ones who understood what we were going through. But then Clay met you. And I finally wasn't getting phone calls at three in the morning about grief, I was getting calls about how he was desperately in love with a woman in group therapy and he wasn't even sure she knew his name."

More laughter. Giselle rests her head on Clay's shoulder.

"It was meant to be. There's nothing else to say about it. So, take care of my buddy. And Clay, you and I know what it's like to lose everything. So just cherish it. Every second. You know?"

Clay's eyes harden in mine and he nods.

"I love you, man"

He smiles. *I love you*, he mouths.

Not for long, probably. I raise my glass of champagne in the air. "To Giselle and Clay."

The room toasts and claps excitedly. Not bad, not bad. I pass the mic back to DJ who announces, "And now, we'll hear from the Maid of Honor and daughter of the groom, Rye Linden."

Rye rises from her seat as I return to mine. She keeps her eyes down, but I can tell she's nervous from the tense way she holds her shoulders. She joins the DJ on the dance floor and takes the mic. "Thank you," she says into the mic.

It gives feedback and she winces before trying again. "Is this better?"

"Woo!" Giselle cheers. "Go, Rye!"

Rye laughs and blushes. She runs her hand errantly down the front of her dress, smoothing the fabric, no doubt self-conscious about showing. "Well, to say I was honored to be Giselle's maid of honor is an understatement. The most stressful, anxiety-inducing honor of my life, but... "

The guests all chuckle. I have to check myself from smiling too lovingly at her. She's so utterly charming.

"An honor, nonetheless," she says and then checks the paper she's holding. It trembles in her hand. Poor thing isn't used to getting up in front of people and speaking. "Giselle. I'm so glad that my father found you. Though the circumstance of your meeting was born of tragedies, the love that has grown from them makes me believe that you two were meant to be."

Giselle and Clay exchange a loving look.

"After we lost Mom, I couldn't have conceptualized my dad moving on. But when I met you, I realized that the concept of moving on does not mean to 'move on from' but to 'move on with'. There's no world in which my dad or I move on from my mother. But there is a world where we move on with the love she instilled in us and give it to others."

Rye isn't speaking to me, but it feels like she is. It's as if she's invoked Rose in this moment, along with her mother. There is no moving on from. Just moving on *with.* I like that. I want that. I want to propagate the love Rose grew with abandon. Not hold it in.

"Thank you for accepting our weird love language of pizza bagels, *Murder She Wrote* reruns, and driving up to the Trader Joe's in Evanston because the parking is easier."

Giselle grins, eyes full of tears.

"You're my best friend. Seriously," Rye says adamantly. Then, her eyes turn to Clay and I swear, both of them are about to burst into tears full out, right here, in front of all the wedding guests. "Daddy—"

Clay breaks first but doesn't look away from her. Giselle rubs his back, their hands interlaced.

"I know I'm not perfect."

My heart tightens.

"I've always tried my best."

She must be talking about us. Her biggest mistake probably ever.

"But thank you for loving me no matter what." Rye looks back down at her paper and then folds it up. "I wrote more, but I can't." A tear escapes her eyes. "No, my makeup, I can't—"

The wedding guests laugh sympathetically.

"Anyway, I love you both so much. To Daddy and Elle."

I'm too stunned to partake in the toast. What have I done? I've ruined this whole day for her. It's always been just as much for her as it's been for Giselle and Clay. And I've spoiled it by letting my impulses get the best of me.

Of course, it takes two to tango. But I'm older. I'm supposed to be more mature. I should have stopped it or insisted we use a condom at the very least, what the hell is wrong with me?

Rye returns to her seat, but not before Giselle and Clay embrace her and pepper her face with kisses. Still treating her like a little girl. Little do they know that their little girl is about to do the womanliest thing a person can do.

"Those were both just perfect," Giselle says to both of us as she sits back down. "I couldn't have asked for better."

"I'm not short, Ash," is Clay's first response.

"Fine. Your vertically challenged."

"Boys... " Giselle says, grabbing both our wrists. Then she throws Rye a look. "Can't live with 'em... can't live without 'em."

Rye tries to smile, but clearly is still trapped in her emotions. God, I can't imagine how she's feeling. She's probably wishing that her mother was here.

The rest of the meal, Clay attends to the women of his life, doting on Rye and Giselle every moment. I'm able to get into a conversation with some of the groomsmen over nothing in particular. Not a moment goes by that I'm not overly aware of Rye and what she's doing or what she's saying.

I won't rush it.

My moment will come.

* * *

"Let's invite the couple onto the dance floor for the first dance as man and wife," DJ announces.

Finally. It's time.

Everyone gathers around the dance floor as Giselle and Clay meet in the middle. Rye stands on the opposite side of the circle from me. She's doing that nervous tick, running the pendant of her necklace back and forth, back and forth.

I'm not nervous. I've steeled my nerves. I'm ready to have her in my arms.

The band launches into a rendition of 'How Deep Is Your Love' that is both corny and wonderful at the same time. Giselle and Clay do a fine job, enjoying themselves, laughing, finding moments of closeness. They're so in love it makes me jealous.

"Now, we'd like to invite the maid of honor and best man onto the dance floor," DJ announces.

I look across the dance floor at Rye and *finally*, she looks back. Her expression is... despondent. Sad. It breaks my heart. I'd love to fix it. But I also know it's because of me.

I take a few strides onto the dance floor and wait for her to meet me. "I've been practicing. Promise I won't embarrass you."

Rye can't hold back a giggle; she looks to Celia, who stands beside her with a nervous smile. The older woman nudges her onto the dance floor, forcing her to walk toward me.

As soon as we meet, the song changes. Something groovier, if that were possible, but slower, with a thick, plodding bass. Something by the Pointer Sisters, I think. I hold out my hand to her and she takes it. My whole body lights up. I've missed her touch. I've had so little of it in my life, and yet I haven't stopped craving it since that first time.

We assume a dancing position, her hand on my shoulder, mine on her waist. The pang in my heart comes on as strong as it's been. Right there. My baby. Our baby.

As if she's reading my mind, Rye speaks first. "I liked your speech."

"Nothing compared to yours," I say with a small smile.

Rye smiles and looks away, eyes on our feet.

I look over her shoulder at the crowd and find my boys all staring wide-eyed. They all give me thumbs ups. *Subtle, guys. Really subtle.* But it's just the encouragement I need. "You look beautiful," I say as meaningfully as I can.

Rye looks up at me for only a moment.

"Haven't been able to take my eyes off of you."

She smiles sadly. "I know."

Now it's me who turns my gaze away. The embarrassment of being known is heavy on my mind. I can't contain a flush. Thank God Clay and Giselle are already on the dance floor, completely wrapped up in each other and now, the rest of the wedding party is trickling out around us. I have a million questions for her. How is she feeling being first and foremost, but I feel like that'd just make things worse.

Instead, I tighten my grip on her, bring her closer to me. She doesn't resist, even if her eyes widen slightly. I subtly rub my thumb against her waist. *I'm here.*

"We'd like to open the dance floor to anyone willing to get down and be groovy on this righteous night... " DJ announces, much to my chagrin.

I feel her pull away from me. I can't stop her. But I can try. "Rye... "

Her blue eyes tremble into mine, filling with tears. She shakes her head the slightest bit and forces a smile.

Not here. Not now. I'll respect that, even if it breaks my heart. I let go of her and take a step back. And without another look or word, Rye turns and disappears into the crowd.

Tomorrow. Tomorrow, I'll make it known. I won't ruin Clay's wedding today, wont' ruin it for any of them. But tomorrow is a new day.

Tomorrow, she'll be mine.

Chapter 23

Rye

I lean out the window of my Uber and wave at Dad and Giselle. "Bye! Have the best time on your honeymoon!"

"Call us when you get to the airport! And when you're on the plane! And when you—" Dad starts.

"Call us when you're in Madison!" Giselle cuts him off, clutching his arm tightly.

He looks at her appreciatively. Despite partying hard last night, they both are in good spirits. Tonight, they're heading off on their honeymoon. Two weeks of tropical bliss. I'm almost jealous, but the thought of being in a beautiful destination when I feel as constantly nauseated sounds awful.

I blow them a final kiss and then roll up the window. "Ready," I tell the driver and off we go, toward O'Hare.

I pull out my phone, take a deep breath, and call Dara. "On my way."

"Eeee! I can't wait," Dara squeals into the phone. "I'm going to give you the biggest hug when you get here."

"Well, be careful. I might puke on you."

"Oh god, is it that bad?"

I shake my head. "Not bad, just unpredictable."

Dara hesitates. "It's all going to be worth it."

I smile to myself and touch my stomach. "Yeah, You're right." Now that I'm officially on my way to Madison, it feels like I'm really taking the next step into this part of my life. Into my version of motherhood. Doesn't look as I'd pictured or as I'd hoped. But... it's happening.

"Tell me about the wedding. How was it? You looked amazing from the pictures you sent."

I cleared my throat. "Well, it was lovely. You know, save one little hiccup, it was a beautiful wedding."

"By little hiccup, do you mean 'big, handsome hiccup'?"

"Dara."

Dara sighs, "I'm sorry! You can't tell me he didn't look good, though."

Of course, he looked good. He looked so fucking fine I was wet the whole night. It doesn't help that being pregnant has already sparked my libido. "He looked good. And that's the long and short of it."

"Okay, I won't ask anything more about it. But you're always welcome to give me more details..."

I laugh. "I'll keep that in mind."

"So, listen, the bakery's all set. First day is next Monday. Sound good?"

I look out the window at Chicago rolling past me. My heart hurts a bit. I was so excited to get back and I'm already saying goodbye. "You're the best, Dara. Seriously."

"Don't say that *yet*. You haven't seen the state of my pantry."

"We'll work on it," I chuckle.

We chat until I get to O'Hare. "I'll be there when you land," Dara says before she hangs up.

My heart swells. I'm not alone in this. Dara's been here every second since I told her. I'm going to make it. I'm going to make it work.

However, this feeling doesn't last long. As I make my way through security and weave through the terminal to my gate, my excitement fades. I'm tired. So tired. And I'm barely pregnant. I'm not even big yet. I'm just exhausted.

Not long after I arrive at the gate, we board. Once I'm settled into my seat, I feel nauseous from the smell of someone's perfume. I pull my sweatshirt up around my face and stare out the window at the air traffic control workers milling about outside the plane. I can see the wing, its metal edge glinting in the sunshine. I'm hit with a wave of emotion. Tears well into my eyes.

I'm leaving. I'm saying goodbye. When I tell my dad I'm pregnant, it will be over the phone. He'll have to come visit me in Wisconsin probably. He'll have questions.

I've only known a month and I'm already tired of lying.

My baby... this is Ashton Hawthorn's baby.

The plane starts to back up onto the tarmac and quicker than usual, we're revving for takeoff, speeding down the runway until I can no longer hear the pavement under the wheels. It's just air now. I watch Chicago get smaller and smaller. Daddy, Giselle, Ash...

I touch my belly. "You and me. It's you and me," I whisper to myself. But as much as I try to remind myself that I'm not alone, I have a hard time believing it.

Tears have started streaming down my face without me even realizing. And as soon as the plane breaks through the clouds and Chicago is completely obscured beneath us, I say the words I couldn't last night.

"Goodbye, Ash."

Chapter 24

Ash

I don't know if flowers are a good idea, but I felt like I should bring something. I'm standing outside of Clay's house, bouquet in hand, about to tell Rye how I feel about her.

This could go very poorly.

I do not have another choice, though. I snuck out of the wedding early last night, unable to continue looking at her having fun and exchanging laughter and smiles with everyone but me. But even without her in front of me, Rye didn't leave my mind for a second.

I want to be there for her. For our child. There's got to be something better than this.

I ring the doorbell. No going back now.

The door flies open. It's Giselle, smiling through a confused face. "Ash! What a surprise!"

"May I come in?" I ask.

"Of course, of... " Her eyes go to the flowers and then to me. maybe she's confused why I'm not offering them to her. "Clay! Ash is here!"

Shit. I don't have a chance to tell her my intentions

before Clay appears in the hall, buttoning the cuff of his shirt. "Ash! What a surprise. These for me?" he says in a joking voice.

I'm in no mood to joke. "No."

"Okay," he frowns. Giselle and Clay look at one another and then at me. "You here to see us off for the honeymoon? You're a little early. Our flight's not until six tonight."

"No, I'm... I'm here to see Rye."

Clay scoffs and crosses his arms. But Giselle's eyes widen. She's already catching on. "Rye? What do you want with Rye?"

I swallow. This is happening now whether I like it or not. "I think we should sit," I say quietly.

"Ash, what's going on?" Giselle asks. She wraps her hand around Clay's bicep. Anticipating.

"Could we sit first?" I reiterate.

Clay furrows his brow. "Ash. What do you want with Rye?"

Okay. This is happening. No sitting. "I owe her an apology."

"For what?" Clay asks.

"For... well for a lot of things, but—"

"What the hell is going on?" he interrupts.

Giselle pulls on his arm. "*Clay*."

"I'm in love with her," I blurt.

Silence all around. Clay and Giselle stare at me with wide eyes. Clay starts to laugh, breaking the silence, "Is that some kind of joke?"

I look at the flowers and then back at him.

"Okay, Ash was right, we should sit... " Giselle tries to pull him into the living room, but Clay isn't budging.

"You're joking, right?"

I purse my lips. "No, I'm not."

Clay takes a step toward me. "Well, you can't tell her. Because she doesn't feel the same way. And you can just forget it, okay?"

"Clay—"

"No. I'm serious, Ash. I don't know what kind of story you've made up in your head, but that's not happening," he says, trying to smile even though his voice could cut like a knife.

"It's already happened," I say.

His jaw twitches. "What does that mean?"

"I mean... it's... we've already... " I take a deep breath. "We tried not to."

"Oh my god," Giselle mutters, covering her mouth.

Another step toward me. "You tried not to *what*?" Clay asks.

"Clay... " I say. "I'm in love with your daughter. And it's not just coming from nowhere, it's... we've... connected."

Clay's mouth falls open, but he doesn't say anything.

"And I need to see her. To tell her that I love her because I'm—" Fuck, I'm going to say it. I'm really going to tell him. "She's pregnant with my baby."

The moment it comes out of my mouth, I'm struck by how much my life suddenly feels like a soap opera. The twists, the turns, the drama. How the fucking hell did I get here?

This musing is cut short by a fist connecting with my jaw. I can't say I don't deserve it.

Pain cuts through the lower half of my face. The flowers fly from my hand. Giselle screams. I catch myself on the entryway table, gasping for air. My mouth tastes like metal. Blood. He better not have broken any of my teeth.

I spit into my hand, red coating the inside of my palm. "Jesus fucking Christ," I groan.

I don't have a moment to retaliate before I feel a knee to the groin. I gasp, breath knocked out of me, a sharp stab cutting through my groin. I fall to my knees, collapsing to the ground, every pump of my heart sending another searing pain through me.

"Be thankful I don't castrate you instead."

"Clay, *stop!*"

I look up, vision blurred, only able to make out the outlines of Giselle holding Clay back.

"What is wrong with you?!"

"Me? What's wrong with him?! He—"

"I know he did, but this isn't what Rye would want, you know that."

I can see clearly now, the pain dulling further and further. I try to catch my breath.

"How the hell would we know what Rye would want? She didn't even... " Clay's anger starts to fade. His eyes waver. "Why didn't she tell me? Why'd I have to hear it from him?"

"Probably because she was afraid you kick her in the balls," I mumble.

He glares at me. "You want me to do it again?"

"Boys! Stop it!" Giselle cries out, stepping between us. She gives me her hand, helping me up from the ground.

"Thank you," I murmur, massaging my jaw and bracing myself on the entryway table. I still feel unbalanced, a wreck from the sudden beating I got from Clay.

She stays between us. I know if she wasn't there, he'd lunge at me again. He's like a hungry predator in a cage, waiting to be fed.

"Okay. Explain it to us, Ash," Giselle says.

"How can you be so calm?" Clay asks sharply.

She rolls her eyes. "Because I could tell something was

going on." Then she looks at me, her brown eyes strong and cutting. "I just didn't know what."

I lick my lower lip. "Could we sit *now*?"

We make our way into the living room, me practically limping and Clay stalking like a wild animal. Thank God for Giselle's level headedness. Otherwise, I would have hit him right back. As soon as I'm settled on the couch, Clay stares me down. "Talk."

"I can only tell you how I feel. I can't assume Rye's side of things. But... from the moment I saw her when I picked her up to go tour the venues, I felt something for her. I barely even recognized her from all those years ago. So, when I found out it was *Rye...* " I trail off and look away. "I knew I couldn't do anything."

Clay chews on his lower lip threateningly. Feels like he could eat me.

"Go on," Giselle says.

I smile at her in thanks. "But we had to spend all this time together. To plan the wedding."

"Don't act like it's *my fault*," Clay spits.

"I didn't say that, I just—"

"You wanted to hear the story," Giselle says, grabbing Clay's hand. "Let him talk."

Clay leans back on the opposite sofa and looks out the window. He's listening, but he won't grace me with his attention. Fine.

"We talked so much, we learned so much about each other. We connected over losing Rose and Heather. There was a spark. And once we acknowledged it, we agreed we couldn't do anything about it because of you. We didn't want to hurt you, Clay. I promise."

He still won't look at me. But I have Giselle's complete

attention. She's watching me, sitting tall and elegant, not backing down from the truth.

"But we just couldn't... stop. And then she... "

Clay's eyes shut tightly. "Please, don't."

"She found out about the baby," Giselle finishes my sentence. Clay visibly winces, putting his face in his hand.

I nod solemnly. "I didn't react like I should have. It was so unexpected. I know I hurt her. I've tried to make it up to her, but she hasn't let me and now I—"

"I can't listen to this," Clay mutters.

"Look, man, the last thing I wanted to do was hurt you. But you have to listen to me when I tell you that I really, really love her. And I never thought I could have that again; you know I didn't."

He looks at me finally. The rims of his eyes are red.

"You have your second chance. I want it too. And I'm sorry that I feel it's with Rye. Believe me, I would not have chosen that for myself."

"Well, you'd be so lucky to have Rye," he says coldly.

I nod. "Yes, absolutely, I just meant... I just need to see her. And find out if she feels the same way. Because if she does, I'll take care of her. I'll take care of our baby. You know I'm good for that, don't you?"

Clay doesn't respond. Giselle looks at him expectantly. "Clay... "

"Why aren't you mad?" he asks her. "Aren't you mad that he—"

"How can I be mad if it made Rye happy?" she replies.

Man, I owe Giselle a dozen bouquets after this. *At least.*

"Well, how could we possibly know that? She's gone," Clay says.

I furrow my brow. "What are you talking about?"

"She moved back to Madison this morning."

I feel the blood drain from my face. "What?"

"Didn't you know?"

I shake my head. "No, I didn't know. I didn't... when did she decide to do that?"

"The decision was pretty sudden," Giselle says, her eyes falling to the ground. "Makes sense now that we know she's—"

"Don't say it," Clay interrupts. "I can't bear to think about it."

I start to breathe heavily. "When did she leave?"

Giselle answers, "Just a few hours ago. Her flight was—"

"Oh my god," I say and get to my feet. My pulse is racing, I can't keep still. I start walking back and forth. "She's gone, she's fucking gone. What the fuck, what the fuck?"

"Okay, easy, just breathe," Giselle says in her smooth voice.

I can't breathe, though. "I can't believe this is happening again."

"What's happening again?" Clay asks.

"I'm losing the love of my life *again*!" I yell. "Don't you see? I lost Rose because I fucked up and now, I've lost Rye, because I—"

"You didn't fuck up. Rose died in a car accident," he cuts me off. "I won't let you go down that road."

I shake my head and cover my eyes. "It's happening again. I'm doing it *again*."

Suddenly, I feel a hand on my back. Not Giselle this time, but Clay. "It's *not* happening again."

I lose it. Break down into sobs right there into my hands. Clay pulls me into his chest; we do not speak for a long while. "She's not dead. She's just in Wisconsin."

I can't help but laugh. And neither can he. And neither

can Giselle. We all laugh. She's just in Wisconsin. A state away. I can still fix this. "Do I have your blessing to go after her?" I ask, putting my hands on my friend's shoulders.

"I fucking hate your guts."

"I know."

"And if I cut off your balls, you'd deserve it."

"Definitely."

Clay takes in a deep breath. "But I think it's pretty obvious how much you care for her."

I smile though a few tears spill down my cheeks. He's the only man I can cry in front of without any shame. We've both done it so many times over the years dealing with the deaths of our wives.

"So, go to her. And if she loves you back, then... " Clay looks off and then nods. "Then good."

We embrace each other again tightly. Giselle encircles us both in her arms. "Aw, my boys! Look at you!"

"She's staying with her friend Dara. I have her address. I'll text it to you," Clay says as we release each other.

I thank them both profusely, especially Giselle who gives me a huge hug and whispers, "I'm glad it's you." It fills my heart.

I'm glad it's me too. Now, all she has to do is choose me.

Too bad that's completely out of my control.

Chapter 25

Rye

"Welcome home!" Dara cries out as she flings open the door.

I smile as big as I can even though the thought of this being my home now sends a lightning bolt through my middle and splits me in two. The apartment opens up into a living room with a pull-out couch that's already all made up with bedclothes. There is exposed brick all around, tall windows with afternoon light streaming in, and all of Dara's homey touches: a candle burns on the kitchen counter, something that smells like an overly sweet cupcake.

"Oh, shit, totally forgot to blow that out before I left to pick you up. Yikes!" she says through a bubbly laugh and rushes to blow it out.

I drop my backpack on a chair and take a deep breath. It's small. But it'll do for now. Besides, it's so good to see Dara. Her beautiful smile, her skeins of blonde hair, her warm hazel eyes. I've always felt really safe with her. And now, more than ever, I need to feel safe.

"I'll take the pull-out couch. You can have my bed,"

Dara says, leaping onto the rickety pullout. The springs creak with her weight.

I shake my head. "Dara, that's ridiculous."

"Um, you think I'm letting you sleep on a pullout couch in your condition? Dream on!"

My condition. I know she's saying it in a tongue-in-cheek way, but all it evokes to me is the image of me unable to get out of bed from the weight of my pregnant belly, made even worse by a pullout couch with no lumbar support. I already had lower back pain before being pregnant. Now, I'm totally fucked.

"I know it's not much..." she says as I dissociate into the future. "But it's going to be great. The two of us. And the lease is up in a couple months, we can find a bigger place for us and the baby."

That sets something off. I don't even know anymore how to control it. But I burst into tears.

"Oh my god! Oh no! Rye!"

"I'm sorry! I don't know why I'm crying! I can't help it!"

Dara wraps her arms around me. "I know why you're crying. It's all a lot. And your hormones—"

"It's not just the hormones," I weep.

"No, of course not," she coos and pats my back.

She lets me cry into her arms for a while, neither of us saying anything. Eventually, Dara pulls away and pushes my hair out of my face. "Oh, Rye. This has to be so hard."

"No, it's just—"

"*Rye,*" Dara interrupts firmly. "It has to be so hard."

I haven't let myself think that thought. If I did, I was sure it would scare me. But the moment I decide to believe it, that the circumstances that have befallen me are *hard*, my entire body relaxes. "It is. I'm so scared."

"I know. Me too!" she says through a smile. "But it's

going to be so worth it. Right? There's a reason you're keeping the baby."

I smile through my tears. She's right. There's a reason for all of this. I could have just... taken care of it. But I know that on the other side of all this pain and frustration is the next, most important part of my life. "You're right."

"I know I am. And I'm sorry, but *fuck* Ashton Hawthorn."

I snort and roll my eyes. "Dara... "

"Fuck him! I don't care if he freaked out. He's a fucking forty-five-year-old man!"

"Forty-six."

"Even worse!"

Even though my world as I've known it is crumbling, I can't help but laugh. Dara just brings it out of me.

"Come on. Tomorrow, we're going to do all the things we used to do in Madison. Visit all our spots. You can see the bakery. But today? Today it's just you and me. And the little one. And ice cream. And crappy movies. And fried food. Sound good?"

I smile. "That sounds *really* good."

"Just like old times," she says and then leans down to my stomach. "Except with a new friend!"

I laugh. I have mourned quietly not being able to share my changing body and my growing baby with Ash. I won't have someone to worship my body and marvel at the changes. But the way Dara is acting, it seems like that won't be a problem at all.

"Okay, let me go get your bags from the car and—"

"I'll go with you."

"No! Nope. You're not lifting a finger today," she says, waving me off. "You rest."

Dara is out the door and down the stair before I have

time to quibble. I go take a seat on the edge of the pullout bed. I'm exhausted. The past six months have been... well, a whirlwind to say the least. Planning a wedding, sleeping with Ashton Hawthorn, getting pregnant with his baby, *attending* said wedding, moving back to Madison, and now?

I don't know what's next. All I know is that in about seven months, I'm having a baby. That's a fucking terrifying thought.

* * *

The afternoon quickly turns to night. Dara and I have snuggled up on the couch with movies on in the background, blankets out the wazoo, and enough snacks to last through the apocalypse. For the most part, we chat through the whole movie. I tell her about everything going through my head. She has lots of questions that I haven't yet answered. So, I fill her in.

"I'm sorry, all I'm doing is talking about myself," I mutter with a sigh.

"Honey, you need to talk about yourself. There's a helluva lot going on."

"Tell me about what's going on with you. Just a little. It will help me... " I trail off and then gesture to my brain. "Help me get out of my own head."

Dara shrugs and leans her head onto the back of the couch. "Well, there's not a lot going on with me. At least not compared to you!"

"*Great*," I say dryly.

"You know what I mean! You've had a lot to think about, Rye. I'm just doing my usual thing. I work at the bakery, I read a lot of books, I see friends occasionally. I don't know. I'm kind of boring."

I smile. Even though she's only five years younger than me, that difference is pretty significant in your twenties. "No guys?"

She makes a disgusted face. "I mean, not lately."

"What's that face?"

"Well, I had this one guy on tap and—"

"'On tap'?"

She blushes. "Yeah, I mean, for hookups and things. But he kind of wanted more and I just... I don't have time for that."

"Oh, Dara."

"Don't 'Oh, Dara' me, Rye," she replies. "I'm busy. I've got a lot going on."

"You just said that you spend a lot of your time *reading*!"

"What's wrong with that?"

I laugh. "Fair."

Dara shakes her head. "Guys just aren't a part of my life right now. I've got time to figure that out, don't you think?"

Twenty-four years old is so young. Even though I'm just twenty-nine and feel like a baby having a baby, twenty-four feels *infantile*. "Yeah, you do."

We're interrupted by a knock at the door. We exchange a look.

"Are you expecting someone?" I ask.

"Um. No. It might be one of my neighbors, though. They're always asking me for a cup of sugar. I'm like, 'Just cause I'm a baker doesn't mean I always have a cup of sugar on hand,'" she says, heaving herself up from the pullout couch.

I look at her expectantly. "But you always do, don't you?"

"Of course, I do, I'd be psychotic not to."

The knock comes again.

"Coming! I'm coming! Relax! I have sugar!"

I laugh and lean back on the couch, turning my attention to the movie, subconsciously moving my hand to my stomach. This life isn't so bad.

Dara opens the door and is immediately met with a deep, staggering voice: "I'm looking for Rye."

I know that voice. I know it so well that it's haunted my dreams since I was sixteen.

Ash.

Chapter 26

Ash

The little blonde girl looks at me like I have two heads. "What do you want with Rye?"

"Dara. It's okay."

I look over the girl's shoulder and immediately feel warmth enter my body: Rye. I've found her. Her brown hair is piled on top of her head in a messy bun, she wears a T-shirt and sweatpants, and no makeup at all, and I swear she's never looked more beautiful. This day, the trauma, the terror. It's all worth it for this moment.

As soon as I left Clay's house, I called up a pilot I know and drove out to a private hangar in the suburbs where I was able to charter a small plane to get up to Madison as soon as possible. Of course, even with all my money and power, the intricacies of traveling made it impossible to get to Rye as quickly as I would have wanted. The later it got, the more dread I felt.

I've lost her, I've lost her, I've lost her.

And now, I've found her. I brush past the blonde girl and walk into the small apartment toward Rye. Her blue eyes do not leave mine. So unlike the wedding just last night when looking at me seemed painful for her.

"Hello, Ash."

"Hi, Rye."

"Oh my god," the blonde girl, Dara, peeps from behind me.

I can't resist running to her and taking her up in my arms. Rye's body gives into me entirely, allowing herself to be swept up in my embrace. She holds me back. I kiss the side of her head, her cheek, her forehead. "I'm sorry, I'm so sorry, Rye."

"You came for me," she says softly.

"Of course," I reply. "The moment I heard you'd left, I... " I cradle her head in my hands and look into her eyes. I smile down at her. "I had to come find you."

Rye raises up on her tiptoes and kisses me. Her lips are like coming home. We've had each other so few times, and yet, I cannot deny how right it feels to have her in my arms.

"Um. I have to... uh... run to the store. I'll give you two some privacy, okay?" Dara anxiously monologues from the doorway. I hear the jangling of keys, the flurry of moment, and finally, the door closes.

Alone. I have not been alone with Rye in a long time. Last night, our dance didn't count, with all those eyes on us.

"What happened to your face?" she asks as we break the kiss.

I remember the bruise on my chin and run my hand over it. "Oh. Your dad."

"My *dad*?"

"I had to tell him about us to find out where you were. I'm sorry, I know it's—"

"Better you than me," she says with a sad chuckle.

I smile. "Your dad has a mean right hook, let me tell you."

"Wow. Didn't know he had it in him. He's mad?"

I nod. "Well, he was. *At me.* Not you."

Rye stares up at me. This is all moving so fast.

"You okay?" I ask, running my hands down her arms as if to check everything is in the right place.

"Yes."

"You're feeling alright? You're—" My hand brushes her waist softly. I can't bring myself to ask directly about the baby yet. But I haven't been able to stop worrying.

"Everything's fine, Ash," she replies.

I stare into her eyes, drinking every bit of her in that I can. "God, I thought I'd lost you," I mutter. "Come here." I sit her down on the edge of the pull-out bed in the middle of the room. Was this where she was going to stay? To live? I can't bring myself to think too hard about it. The sacrifices she was going to make to have our baby in peace, away from the drama, away from me. It breaks my heart. I wrap my hands around Rye's and stare at how they intertwine. "I'm so sorry. For how I reacted."

"It's okay," she whispers.

"It's not. It's really not," I say, tightening my grip on her hands. "I'm a grown man. In no world was that an appropriate way to respond to news like that." I finally draw my gaze up to hers. Rye looks at me with tenderness. There is no anger there. My heart beats harder. "I thought giving you space was right, but all it did was destroy me. When you didn't respond, I—"

"I'm sorry."

"No, no. I understand why you didn't. You didn't owe me anything after how I left you like that," I go on. "In that time apart from you, I just realized so much. I realized that I adore you. Every part of you."

Her lips curl into a sweet smile.

"I want to be a part of our baby's life. I want to take care of you. Because I love you, Rye Linden. I love you so much. Please give me a chance."

"You love me?" Rye responds in shock.

"I couldn't believe it when I realized it either. Ever since Rose died, I didn't think it would be possible for me to find someone. I didn't let myself. Because her death... it was my fault. At least that's what I've told myself."

She frowns. "How do you mean?"

"I... " I don't tell this story, at least not often. I haven't shared it in years, not since I first told my therapist. It terrifies me what people will think of me when I say it. "I had a lot of business meetings back in the day that ended with me drinking way too much. I was always safe in the knowledge that your dad was always there to come pick me up if I got to a point where I couldn't drive. He would always offer me a room to sleep it off in, so I wouldn't disturb Rose. That night was no different and I ended up drunk at a business meeting once again. Fuck, I was such an idiot back then. But your father was out of town that time. There were no taxi's available, so I called Rose and asked her to come pick me up. I waited for a long time... " She knows how the story ends. Car crash. Killed on impact. "If she hadn't been driving that night—"

"Ash. You couldn't have known."

"I should have."

Rye lays a hand over mine. "You couldn't have. Could never have."

Everyone has always tried to reject the guilt I feel for Rose's death. It's still something I have to get over. Hearing

Rye's encouragement makes it seem a little bit more possible now. "That's what I've always told myself, anyway. And because I blamed myself for her death, how could I deserve a second chance? I'd already had the love of my life and I'd lost it... And then in you came, with your beautiful eyes and your kindness and your bubbly laugh and—"

Rye lets out her signature laugh and it fills my heart to the brim.

"Yes. That one."

She flushes, looking away bashfully. I pinch her chin and guide her face back toward mine so I can see her glimmering eyes. "I didn't want it to be true at first. That's why when you told me about the baby, I was so terrified. I didn't know how I could let things get to this point. And as soon as you were gone, I regretted everything. I... " I feel my body growing weak with the memory of this morning, of her father telling me she was gone. "I thought I'd done it again. I'd lost the person I loved and it was all my fault."

Rye's eyes waver in mine. "You really love me?"

"Yes. So much. With every fiber of my being. I love you. I love our baby."

She bursts into tears. Poor thing. I let her bury her face in my chest. I hold her, softly kiss the crown of her head. She wraps her hands around my back, her palms flush against my shoulder blades. "Oh, Ash... "

"I hope you can forgive me."

"Of course, of course," she sobs and then looks up at me once more. Eyes red and puffy, lips smiling through the tears. "I love you too."

I don't entirely believe that after everything I've done that she could love me back. But I won't fight it. I'll let her. Because I love Rye Linden with every fiber of my being. "Really?"

"Yes."

"*Really*, really?"

"Yes, yes."

I can't hold back anymore. I kiss her firmly on her lips, deepening the kiss until our tongues are dueling for dominance. I cannot get enough of her. I thread my fingers through the knot of her hair and ever so gently work the hair tie from her hair so that her dark locks fall around her face.

"Make love to me, Ash," she whispers against my mouth.

"Oh my god... " All the primal feelings I've felt since meeting her again all those months ago return, except this time, they are not unwieldy and aggressive. This woman is carrying my baby. I want to take care of her the best way I can.

"Please."

"Of course, baby. Let me take care of you. Let me show you how I can take care of you."

Softly, I lean her back onto the creaking pullout couch. Reminds me of all the times Rose and I had to quietly have sex in our childhood bedrooms, making sure we weren't overheard. Now, though, I'm a grown man. I don't care who hears. I don't care who knows that we belong to one another. I press a line of kisses up her throat, relishing the long moan she lets out. I run my hand up the inside of her thigh. Her whole body stiffens at my touch. I've missed everything about her. The way she responds to my touch, the sounds she makes, the way her body feels like it belongs to me.

And does it ever now.

"Let me see you, Ash."

I pause.

"Let me see your body."

We've never seen each other naked, at least not soberly. The only time was months ago now, the night of our baby's conception, wine drunk in the dead of night. That doesn't count. I slough off my jacket and then slowly undo the buttons on my shirt. Rye watches with bated breath.

"You're enjoying this," I say with a smirk.

"Absolutely," she giggles. "Every second."

With my shirt undone, I let it fall off my arms. "Your turn."

She reciprocates, pulling her T-shirt over her head, revealing her breasts to me. They're a bit bigger now, the nipples darker. She sees I'm staring at them and touches them delicately with her hands. "They're getting tender."

"I'll be gentle," I respond, leaning down and bestowing a gentle kiss to each breast. "Promise."

Rye smiles and cups my chin in her hand, the scruff rubbing against the inside of her palm. "Now. Your pants."

Chapter 27

Rye

"Yes, ma'am."

I smile as I watch Ash pull his pants down, releasing his cock from its constraints. What a beautiful sight he is. His well-shaped chest covered in dark hair, the v of his hips, his swollen dick standing at full attention. The head is red, looking incredibly tender. I reach for it, wrap my hand around his length, and tug on it. Ash drops his head back with a dreamy sigh and a bead of precum appears on the tip of his cock. "Fuck, Rye."

"Take these off. I want to feel you," I say, thrusting my hips into the air.

"Don't have to tell me twice."

He tugs my sweatpants off and now, we are both completely naked. I lean up onto my elbows, dipping my head back. "Kiss me."

Ash leans down and kisses me. My whole body ignites. Fuck, I'm so much more sensitive now that I'm pregnant. My clit is already throbbing and he hasn't even done anything.

"Get on top of me, baby," he commands.

And why would I say no to that?

We roll over onto the pull out, the springs groaning angrily at us. Neither of us can help laugh. "Feels like I'm in college again," I say with a shake of my head.

"Let's make this quick, I've got an economics exam in the morning," Ash says, pinching the thickness of my ass.

I laugh and pepper his face with kisses and then move my lips down to his clavicle. I trace the outline of his collarbone, gently bobbing my hips over his, so his cock nestles between the lips of my pussy.

"Holy shit, Rye. You're so wet."

"I'm so horny for you."

"I can tell." Ash guides my head up from his chest, he ruffles my hair softly, green eyes examining my every feature. "Do what you need, baby. I want you to feel good."

I already feel good with him hard between my thighs, his naked form underneath me. And to top it all off, he loves me. That thought alone sends a pulse of arousal through me.

"Ride me, honey," he whispers.

I reposition my hips, put Ash at my entrance, and sink down on to his cock. His breath halts: he lets out a long groan, "Holy fuck... "

Every time I've had sex with Ash, it's felt amazing. Somehow, this time, it feels even better. It feels monumental, feels... religious. I rock my hips back and forth until I've taken his entire length into me. The head of his cock knocks up against my cervix and I moan with each thrust.

"You're so sensitive right now, huh?" Ash asks.

I can only nod and whimper.

"Enjoy it, good girl. Enjoy it... " Ash reaches up and begins to massage my tits. When he pinches my nipples, it sets my pelvis alight. What is happening to me? I know that pregnant women can be hornier than usual, but this is...

Fucking amazing.

I ride faster and faster, each pulse driving me higher and higher and there doesn't seem an end in sight.

Ash's hand slinks down from my chest to my belly. "You're mine, Rye," he huffs.

Pleasure spiders down from my hand to my clitoris. I jerk. "Fuck... "

"Everyone will know you're mine."

I start to shake. My thrusts become more erratic. Faster.

"I'll take such good care of you."

"Oh my fucking god... " I groan, my head falling forward.

Ash wraps his other hand around my hip and helps me, pulling me onto his cock over and over. He's so hard, so engorged that each time, my nerves go off like firecrackers. "That's it, baby. That's it."

I shut my eyes tightly.

"Your body is so beautiful."

I drop my head back. My hips are moving so fast they could start a fire. I buck harder and harder until it all becomes too much. Release is imminent. "Fuck, fuck, fuck!" I curse before my entire body shudders. Explosion after explosion inside me; my pussy clenches around his cock so tight he can't avoid coming too. Ash lets out a jittering, ragged shout as he releases his seed into me. The seed I've already taken so well.

His hands try to find purchase on my body wherever they can. His touch is worshipful. I am his goddess, his queen. I can feel it just in the way he holds me.

I collapse forward into his arms, chest to chest with him.

"Oh my god, Rye... you're fucking amazing."

I hum contentedly. "There'll be much more where that came from," I say and kiss his chest. "Promise."

Ash wraps his arms around me, nose against my temple. "My girl."

"Your girl... "

We lay there for quite some time, unspeaking. It's hard to believe how much has changed, just in a single hour. I've gone from feeling bereft and lost to content and found. Life changes on a dime without you even realizing sometimes.

"How long have you loved me?"

"What?" I ask, adjusting my head so I can look in his eyes.

"You said you've loved me a long time," Ash says. He takes a lock of my hair and tucks it behind my ear. "How long?"

I get an intense wave of anxiety at the question. "Oh. That. Well. Don't worry about it."

"No, no, no," he says with a goofy smile. "You can't just say something like that and then not tell me."

I close my eyes. "Ash, it's really embarrassing."

"Hey. You aren't going to lose me. It doesn't matter if you've been in love with me for days or months or... " He pauses and then guffaws, "Years! Although that would be... "

I can't stop from blushing.

Ash's eyes widen. "Years? *Years?*"

"I mean, I wasn't really in *love* with you, I was just a kid."

"Just a *kid*?"

I bury my face in one of the pillows. "You said it doesn't matter whether it was—"

"It doesn't, I promise it doesn't. I'm just... how? Why?"

I sit up and start to busy myself with getting dressed again. "Dara could be back any minute, let's—"

Ash sits up and wraps himself around me from behind. "Rye, honey, I'm telling you, there's literally nothing that could push me away from you." He bestows several kisses to my shoulder. "Just tell me. I want to know."

I sigh. "Okay. Fine. I was sixteen."

"Sixteen?!"

"Stop interrupting!"

Ash seals his lips shut and props his chin on my shoulder. I have to give him credit, he hasn't drawn away from me whatsoever. I just need to come out with it.

"I was sixteen. You know it was right around the time Rose passed away. And you were staying with us while the boys visited their grandparents. In the guest room under the stairs. And one day I was home earlier than usual from my summer classes. And I didn't think anyone was home. But then I heard the shower going in your room and I was confused because I thought you were at the office. So, I went to your room. You had left the door open. And then, on top of the shower running, I heard some weird..." I sigh. "Grunting."

Ash is starting to go red, all the way into the valleys of his dimples.

"And I peeked into your bathroom. And you must not have noticed me, but you were jerking off in the shower," I say and shut my eyes tight with embarrassment. "And I'd never seen that before and I just thought you looked so beautiful; your eyes shut tight, your dick just out and the desperation with which you were trying to come, I mean... "

"Rye Linden, you perv," Ash says teasingly.

I cover my face with my hands. "I know! I know, it's ridiculous!"

"No, I love it. I love it so much. What a compliment. You haven't been able to stop thinking about my dick for years."

I shove him playfully and he holds me tighter. "Anyway, I've never been able to stop thinking about you."

"So, when we had to work together on the wedding—"

"Oh, a nightmare from the jump."

"Wow," he says, biting his lip through a smile.

"You're enjoying this," I grumble.

"Immensely." Ash kisses me. Nothing has changed. Thank God. He's still right here, still kissing me with the same intensity and want as before. "You're the cutest perv I've ever met."

"Ash!!!"

"I'm teasing!" he replies and tucks his lips up near my ear. "I love you, Rye."

I sigh happily. "I love you."

"Come home with me. Come live with me. Make a life with me."

My heart flutters. I can't believe this is real.

"I need you."

There's no question in my mind what my answer is. "Yes. Yes, yes, yes."

Chapter 28

Ash

Three months later

"Watch your step… "

"Ash, I'm just getting out of the car."

"I don't want you to get lost between the car and the curb," I say teasingly, holding out my hand to Rye.

Rye twists her lips and takes my hand. "I wouldn't even fit between the car and the curb at this point," she grunts as she gets out of the car. She smooths her hand down the front of her coat. At six months pregnant, she's really popped. "Thank you," she says with a breathless smile.

Pregnancy is suiting her. The glow hasn't gone away from her face and each day that she grows, she just seems to get more beautiful. I kiss her softly and touch her lower back. "Come on. We're running late."

We make our way inside her obstetrician's office. Since Rye and I reunited back in September, I've been at her side as much as possible, accompanying her to every one of her prenatal appointments. Even though everything's been going well and she's healthy and the baby is healthy, I can't help but feel like a bundle of nervous energy every time.

The waiting room has transformed since the last time we were here with splashes of Christmas décor; twinkling lights around the receptionist's desk, boughs of holly on the walls, a little Christmas tree in the corner. We were lucky to get this appointment in just before Christmas Eve tomorrow.

It's hard to believe we've made it to Christmas. I brought Rye back from Madison with me the very next day and from that moment on, we made our life together. She lives with me in my apartment downtown. We spend a great deal of time with both our families and, even though Clay is still embittered toward me, he's over the moon to become a grandfather. And Giselle's consistent support definitely helps.

It's still a work in progress. After all, the scheme of things, we're still in the puppy love stage. We just have a baby on the way too. That speeds things up. Supporting her through her pregnancy has been an incredibly intimate experience. We can go on a romantic date, have glorious, amazing sex, and the next morning I'm holding her hair while she's morning sick. Our relationship only grows stronger through these moments of vulnerability.

We don't even have a chance to sit down before we are greeted by Dr. Uri. "Rye! Ash! Good to see you, as always."

The three of us go into an examination room. I take Rye's coat while she gets settled and Dr. Uri starts to ask her questions.

"How have you been feeling?" Dr. Uri asks.

"All things considered, I guess good," Rye says, sitting on the edge of the examination table.

Dr. Uri looks at me with a skeptical smile. "Is she being honest, Ash?"

"Don't get me in trouble," I say, clutching my heart.

"I'm getting some bad heartburn," Rye says.

The doctor smiles. "That's super normal. Why don't you lay back for me?"

"It doesn't help that her cravings are—"

"Ash!" she interrupts me with a warning look.

I seal my lips shut but can't help but smile. We've only been together three months and we're already bantering like an old married couple. Our relationship has no doubt been expedited by the pregnancy. I've made myself available to her every waking moment of the day. If I'm at work, I don't hesitate to take a call from her. If she needs something, no matter the time of day, I make it happen.

"Tell me about the cravings, Rye," Dr. Uri says with her friendliest smile.

Rye huffs at me, "You're getting me in trouble."

"Do you want to tell her or do you want me to?" I ask.

She folds her hands over her eyes. "You do it."

I chuckle and brush some hair tenderly from her face. "Burger... extra mayo... extra pickles... "

"I can't help it!" Rye cries out. "I sometimes can't even sleep because I'm thinking about it."

"You're so funny," Dr. Uri smiles. "Okay, pull up your shirt, let's take a look."

Rye pulls up the hem of her shirt, revealing her swollen stomach. She endearingly strokes the bare skin.

"Baby is getting more active too," I say softly.

Rye glances up at me with a tender smile. We've spent hours upon hours lying in bed together, trying to catch every tiny flutter of our baby.

"So, let's see how baby is doing," Dr. Uri announces.

Even though I already have three children, ultrasounds haven't lost their magic. I take Rye's hand in mine when she winces at the cold gel on her stomach and watch the screen intently as Dr. Uri drags the wand around her belly, looking for the fuzzy outline of the baby.

"There's baby!"

Our baby looks like a baby now. Button nose, little hands, pouty lips. My eyes well with tears.

"Ash, don't cry," Rye says, squeezing my hand.

"I can't help it," I sniff.

"Now, I know you said last time you wanted to be surprised by the gender. Is that still the case?" Dr. Uri asks.

I glance at Rye. We had agreed early on that we wouldn't learn the gender ahead of time. I made the mistake of saying I was hoping for a girl and that immediately got in her head. "I don't want you to be disappointed. Once the baby is born, you're just going to be happy they're healthy and you won't even care if it's another boy," she had said the night before her last appointment. She's pretty convinced that we'll have a boy too.

She hesitates to respond to Dr. Uri. I know she wants to know. Rose and I knew with all of our boys before they were born (although they told us Keifer was a girl and look how that turned out). I don't want her not to find out because of me. "Rye, if you want to know—"

"I don't want you to be disappointed if it's—"

"I'm not going to be disappointed," I say and touch her chin gently. "How could I be?"

Rye takes a deep breath and turns her gaze back to Dr. Uri. "Okay. I've changed my mind. I want to know."

Dr. Uri looks at the screen and then between the two of us. "It's a girl."

I feel my heart leap into my throat. I can't believe my ears.

Rye gasps and sits up. "Seriously?"

"Mhm. And she's growing wonderfully. Everything looks great."

"Oh my god, Ash. We're having a girl," Rye says and that's what makes it real.

The tears I reined it at the image of our baby all release at once. I don't have words. And I don't need them. Rye wraps her arms around me, kisses my cheeks, cradles my head to her shoulder. "It's a girl, Ash. It's a girl."

"Our little girl, Rye.." I say. I hold her face in my hands and smile through the tears. I would have been happy with anything, but this just makes it even more clear that we're meant for each other.

* * *

Later that day, I've gone back to the office to finish up some last minute work before the holiday break. I can't focus on anything but my baby. My little girl. I would have been happy with a little boy, but this is just the cherry on top. I'm already thinking of names. Wendy, Colleen, Penelope. I think Rye will hate all of them. They're all very old school. I don't care. I look forward to arguing over the name book for weeks to come.

Everything's moved so fast, but I've been able to keep up. Rye makes it easy. It just proves to me how meant we are for each other.

That thought sets something off at me and before I know it, I'm sitting at my desk, dialing a number I know so well.

"Yellow?"

"You're answering the phone 'yellow' now? How old are you?"

Clay laughs. "Old! I'm about to be a grandfather!"

I smile to myself. The old Clay is right there. He's given me a second chance. And I want to prove to him that I deserve it. "Can I stop by before I head home? I have something I need to ask you about. Something important."

Clay pauses. I think he already knows my question. "Absolutely."

Chapter 29

Rye

I'm just at the precipice of pregnancy where movement is going to start requiring more effort, but luckily, I'm still light on my feet to be able to take care of Christmas dinner.

Ash and I decided to have Christmas Eve dinner up at the house in Wilmette. I wanted it to be a very special gathering for both of our families. We've had several dinners all together over the months, but our first holiday together feels huge.

Giselle and Dad are in charge of cooking, but Ash and I have been helping quite a bit, along with Ash's granddaughter, Piper, who is a pro at licking the spoon.

"What do you think, Pipes?" I ask, holding out a spoonful of mashed potatoes for her to try.

Piper leans forward to take a bite, but Ash intervenes. "Woah, woah, woah! Hold on a second!" He blows on the potatoes to cool them off.

I laugh and nudge Piper's cheek. "Our hero!"

She giggles; I guide the spoon into her mouth. Ash rests

his hand on my lower back. Moments like these with Piper make me anticipate motherhood even more. Especially now that we know we're having a little girl. It feels like we're getting lots of good practice in before our baby arrives. "What do you think?"

"Mmm... yummy," she says with a mouthful of potato.

"Perfect. Then all that's left to get ready is the salad," I call over my shoulder to Giselle and Dad who are standing together at the counter chopping vegetables.

"Heard!" Giselle calls out.

"Ash, why don't you let the boys know they should be ready to start bringing things out into the dining room?" my dad calls out from his place at the counter.

Ash nods. "You got it." Then he kisses my head. "And I'll get this sack of potatoes out of your way." He scoops Piper up into his arms and throws her over his shoulder.

Piper squeals, "Grampa! I'm not a sack of potatoes!"

"A talking sack of potatoes! It's magic!" he cries out and carries her out of the kitchen.

I laugh and touch my belly softly, feeling the baby kick. She already knows what a great daddy she has.

"Rye, honey. Come here," Giselle beckons.

I go meet her at the counter and peer into the salad bowl. It's a flurry of color; spinach, mandarin oranges, radishes. "That looks amazing."

"How are you feeling?" Dad asks, stepping beside me and running a hand through my hair.

"Good. Actually, I want to tell you something," I say with a smile. I've been so excited to tell them that the baby is a girl. Ash is probably telling the boys right now.

Giselle and Dad exchange a look. "We want to tell you something too," she says, wearing a solemn smile.

I frown. "Is everything okay?"

"Oh, it's a good thing, it's not... " Dad takes a deep breath and shakes his head. "You first."

I grin. "I'm having a girl."

They both let out excited yelps, embracing me, kissing me. "Oh, Rye, you must be so excited!" Giselle cries.

"My little girl is having a little girl," Dad whimpers, tears in his eyes.

"Daddy, don't cry."

"I can't help it," he says. He flicks the tears away. "I can't... this is all so much... " Suddenly, he's weeping.

I frown and touch his arm. "Are you upset with me?"

"No, no, of course not, I just... " my dad trails off.

"Rye, we have some news," Giselle interrupts.

I meet her gaze; her warm brown eyes flicker with something. A secret. "What is it?"

"Well... it's surprised even us," she says, a big smile starting to spread on her face.

I feel like I know what she's going to say before she even says that. I look between my dad and Giselle. They're both beaming, glowing. I know that look. I know that feeling. I've had it ever since I found out I was pregnant. "No... "

"I'm pregnant," Giselle says, her voice in an excitable whisper like we're girls talking about our crushes on a playground.

I'm in complete, joyous shock. "How... "

"It just happened, I don't... you know I never thought it would happen naturally, but it did and I... "

My dad lets out a sob into his hands.

"Oh, Daddy. It's okay," I say, wrapping my arm around him.

"I don't want you to think we're stealing your spotlight.

It's still early, but I wanted you to know as soon as we did," Giselle says through a measured breath. It's clearly been weighing heavily on her. I know what it's like to have an uncomfortable conversation like this. After all, when I returned from Madison, I had to sit down with them and explain everything that had transpired from my perspective, had to deal with the heartache my father felt from being left out of this important change in my life. From that very moment, we made an agreement to be completely open and honest, no matter how much it would hurt.

This doesn't hurt at all, though. "Are you kidding? Our babies will be best friends!" I squeak, tears rushing into my eyes. The past six months have been a sob fest for everyone. It's getting boring, but I can't help it. "I'm so happy for you."

Giselle and I embrace; I touch her waist softly. I can feel the energy inside of her, something I think I have only tuned into because of my own pregnancy. The baby flutters in my belly again and Giselle and I both gasp in laughter.

"All my girls together," Dad says and throws his arms around us. He kisses each of our cheeks, touches my stomach gingerly. "Am I lucky or what?"

I smile. We've come so far. I think my dad has had to come to terms with the fact I've watched him be happy beyond his life with my mother, so he's had to step up and get over the weirdness of his best friend being the man I love because *I'm* so happy.

I don't think I've ever had a more special Christmas.

* * *

Christmas Eve dinner is wonderful. The table is full and loud, so much different than the past few Christmases I've had with just Giselle and my dad. Ash and me, Giselle and Dad, Jarred, Oliver, Keifer, his best friend June, Oliver's friends, Rowan and Trevor (an adorable couple if I've ever seen one), and, of course, the queen of us all, Piper. Throughout dinner, I only get more excited for things to come. Next Christmas, we'll have two more babies at the table. Maybe some of the boys will find partners too. And who knows who else will come into our lives?

I have a family. A big, happy family. There's nothing I've ever wanted more.

"The flowers look amazing, Rye," June announces.

"Suck-up," Keifer teases her.

June rolls her eyes. "I'm serious!"

Ash and I exchange a look. The two of them are always giving each other shit, but when I brought up to Ash that I thought there was something there, he said they're apparently just friends. "Thank you," I say with a smile. I reach out and adjust one of the vases of the flowers. The dreams of a flower shop have been put on hold, but not forever. I'll take care of our baby first and then open a shop. Eventually. I'm in no rush. "It's meant to represent the women we've lost. Rose and Heather. Makes for a lovely arrangement."

"That's so beautiful," Rowan says, batting her hauntingly gray eyes. "Isn't it, Trev?"

Ash puts his arm on the back of my chair and gently strokes my arm with one of his fingers. Rose is never far from his mind. I've learned this. I understand it. My mother is never far from mine. Embracing Rose has brought me closer to him. Closer to his boys.

"I have to say," Oliver announces suddenly. "The whole situation is weird. But you two are perfect for each other."

The entire table descends into laughter. "Wow. Thanks, son," Ash says. "You have such a way with words."

I grab Ash's leg under the table and squeeze. His green eyes shoot to mine, pupils dilating the slightest bit. I can't touch this man without him wanting me. Our mutual desire is what brought us together, but my pregnancy has amplified our need. "Later… " I whisper nearly inaudibly.

He leans over and says in my ear, "Wouldn't be the first time we've snuck away to—"

"My dad is right there!" I say and smack him on the chest. But with a glance to my dad, it's clear he's not even worried about us. Just as they were on their wedding day, Giselle and Dad are enamored with each other, basking in the news of their future child. Weird that my dad will have a granddaughter before I'll have a sibling, sure, but it seems our whole family is built on weird now. Who gives a fuck if we're all happy? "I'll take care of you later," I say to Ash.

Ash kisses my temple. "Not if I take care of you first."

Ash's "taking care" comes in the form of a midnight run to a burger joint. Despite the beautiful Christmas Eve dinner, I needed my usual. People always say pregnancy cravings are intense, but they don't really tell you that there are nights you can't *sleep* you need something so bad. Luckily, Ash waits on me hand and foot.

When he walks in the bedroom, face wind burnt from the cold and college sweatshirt mussed, I reach out for the bag from where I set amidst the blankets. "My old friend… you thought I'd forgotten about you," I say.

Ash holds the bag out over my hands, but when I got to grab them, he jerks it away. "What do you say?"

I flush. "Thank you."

"Mhm. At the very least. Making me go out in the cold," he murmurs and kisses me softly.

"You offered," I retort.

"Of course I did." Ash smiles.

I return the smile and take the bag. Relief floods my body. "You probably think I'm a monster," I laugh, taking a few fries out of the bag and chowing down.

Ash laughs and lays down on the bed next to me while I eat. "What the hell are you talking about?" He wraps one of his large hands around my bump and strokes it back and forth softly. My body fills with warmth.

"I was this beautiful younger woman. Now I'm a hungry witch in your bed."

"Rye... "

"Hm?" I hum with a mouthful of my burger.

Ash leans on his elbow. "You're having my baby. You could be covered in mud from head to toe and smell like a sewer and I'd think you're the most perfect woman on Earth."

I smile. I love being pregnant. I really do. I've never felt more special, never felt more important. I've found the exact right man to do this with.

"Plus, I've seen it all before. There's not a lot that takes me off-guard. I'm just out of practice," he says with a smug smile.

"Okay, keep bragging... " I reply.

"No bragging! Just the truth."

There are some days I feel a little sad that he's done this all before. He's not experiencing it all for the first time like I am. But other times, it's so comforting to have him on such an even keel. Not scared, confident that everything that's happening is right. And that makes me confident, allows me to enjoy my changing body and look forward to the future.

"Although, a little girl... " he muses and then puts his mouth up against my belly. "Already spoiling you, aren't I?"

I laugh and run a hand through his dark hair. "Daddy's little girl, for sure."

"I know. I'm totally screwed," he sighs.

I finish up my midnight snack soon after that; Ash cleans up while I settle back into bed. And though I was desperate to eat so that I could fall asleep, I'm not quite tired. Maybe it's the impending Christmas day tomorrow. We have a house full: the boys all in their rooms, the guest rooms full too. Tomorrow morning, we will all get up and snuggle up in the family room in front of the magnificent tree. We'll all watch Piper unwrap all her gifts, delight in her giggling and big green eyes, her kisses and cuddles.

Ash isn't tired either. He lays next to me and touches my stomach, as usual. It never loses its newness, its excitement. "Next Christmas, our little one will be here."

I can't hold back a huge grin. I touch Ash's hand at my waist. "She'll be crawling by then."

"Wow," he utters.

"And guess what?"

His vivid eyes that have been locked on my bump flick up into mine. "What?"

"She won't be the only baby."

Ash's dark eyebrows jump. "Don't tell me you have a secret twin or something."

"No! Oh my god, *no*. That sounds like a nightmare," I laugh.

"Then what are you talking about?!"

I purse my lips and lean closer to him so we're sharing the same pillow. "You can't tell anyone."

"Promise."

"*Ashton.*"

"Don't you trust me?" he asks with a smile, teeth glimmering.

I don't have to answer that. Of course, I do. I don't know if everyone would be able to after the way we started things off. The pain when he rejected our baby, rejected me. But he's made up for it every day since. And I have to say, a man chasing after you across state lines by plane really does wonders for confidence in a relationship. "Giselle and Dad are having a baby."

Ash's face softens, eyes wide. "No."

"Yes! Isn't that exciting?"

"Oh my god. Wow. *Wow*." He turns over and runs his hand through his hair. "That's... they must be so happy."

I snuggle up to him. My belly isn't large enough to make it too difficult yet. "They are."

"And you?" Ash asks, looking back at me and curling his hand through my hair.

"Thrilled. Is that weird?"

He smiles at me sweetly, endeared to me. "No. Not at all."

I kiss him gently and press a hand to his chest, rubbing my thumb back and forth. "It's crazy how fast things change, hm?"

Ash furrows his brow. He looks away for a second. Something's bothering him. His lips twist as if he wants to say something. I wait, not prodding him to tell me. He will. He always does. "Rye."

"Yes, Ash."

"We should be married by next Christmas."

I blink. Not in a million years would I have guessed that's what he was going to say. "Are you proposing?"

"Is it alright if I am?"

I let out an errant laugh. I'm in disbelief. This is definitely not how I thought it'd go down. In fact, even though Ash and I had alluded to the idea of being married just in and around our developing connection, I just didn't foresee it happening for a long time. "Um. Yes. Yes, that'd be alright."

Ash reaches into his nightstand. Does he already have a ring? This is all happening so fast. I sit up in bed, straight as a pole. He holds out a gray box. "I thought I'd do something much more creative, but... "

When he opens it, I'm struck even more dumb than I already am. It's my mother's engagement ring. I thought she'd been buried with it. "How did you... "

"I went to ask your dad for his permission. You know, seems only fair at this point to run things by him."

I laugh and bring my hand up to my mouth, totally gob smacked.

"He's been saving it for you. We can get you a ring if you'd rather, but I—"

"No, no. This is perfect." Of course Dad saved it. Of course he knew I'd want it.

Ash smiles shyly. "Will you marry me, Rye?"

I nod before he's even done with the question. "Yeah. Yes."

We fall into each other's arms before he can put the ring on my finger. I pepper his face with kisses, down his jaw, his neck. I frame his face in my hands, examining every beautiful edge and curve. The indents of crow's feet, the ridge of his cheekbones, his pert bottom lip. "I love you."

He sighs in relief. "I love you more than I ever thought possible."

I kiss him. My whole body alights, so much so that our baby flips inside me. Ash can feel it too; he touches my stomach and smiles into my mouth. "I think that's a good sign," he chuckles.

"I think so too."

Ash slips the ring on my finger; it's a simple gold band with one diamond. Just like my mother and father, simple and practical. Elegant. Everything to me. I twiddle my fingers, marveling at the way it looks on my hand. "Wow... "

"I think we should be married before the baby comes."

I gasp. "Ash!"

"It just seems right. You know. The right way to do things."

"Yes, because we're so good at doing things the right way."

Ash turns red around his nose. "That's why it's important to me that we do things right from now on. For us. For our little girl."

Our little girl... Damn, I like the sound of that.

"We can make it happen fast. Get a planner. You know, money is no object, it won't be a problem to—"

"Ash, I'll be huge by the time we can throw something together," I say, already imagining how much bigger I'll be in just a month.

He grunts. "That's fine, that's—"

"No wedding planner. No big wedding. I want it simple. I want it quick," I say with a smile.

Ash frowns. "You don't want a big wedding?"

"Hell fucking no," I laugh. "Not after the last one."

Ash laughs too. The ups and downs of planning Giselle and Dad's wedding have turned me off of weddings completely. "A big party then."

"Yes. A big party. That's much better," I reply and then take his big hand in mine. His hands that are so strong that will be so tender with our baby. Have been so tender with me. "All I need is you and our families there. We could elope or go to the courthouse. I don't care. Just simple. Clear."

"Clear?"

I lock our hands together, rest them on the ridge of my stomach. "That all I need is you."

Ash smiles big. He lifts my hand to his mouth, finds my ringed finger, and kisses it. "All I need is you, too."

Epilogue

Ash

Three months later...

I'm fit to burst, sitting at Rye's side, watching her holding our baby. Little Ivy. She's been alive for five hours and she's already one of the best things that's ever happened to me.

Rye's dark hair is piled on the top of her head in a big knot and she's completely at peace. You wouldn't even know that she'd been in labor for two days and threatening to castrate me between pushes.

"Look at her hand," she says.

I do. Ivy's little hand curls around Rye's pinky. She pulls it toward her little, ruby mouth, all coated in spit.

"One, two, three, four, five. Okay. Five," Rye mutters. She's counted Ivy's fingers and toes about twenty times already. When Ivy was first laid on her chest, wailing, Rye thought she saw six fingers and started panicking.

I kiss the top of her head. "You want me to take her? Lay her down in the bassinet?"

"No."

"Aren't you tired?" I ask.

Rye looks up at me and grins. "Exhausted."

I smile back. I've had only a couple moments to hold Ivy. I've been very patient. After all, she was inside Rye all these months. I can't imagine what kind of mind fuck that is to finally see her outside and know she's real.

Ivy blinks her scrunched eyes open. They're cloudy right now and I can't tell if they'll be green or blue. Hopefully, the perfect combination of both.

"Hello, Ivy," I say.

Ivy squirms.

"Keep talking to her," Rye encourages.

"I love you."

Ivy burbles, spit appearing on her lips. She lets go of Rye's finger and raises her hand higher. I lean down and let her touch my lips. She explores it tenderly, unsure yet of how to grab, yet desperate to know their feeling. I kiss her hand again and again. "I could just eat you up. Yes, I could."

"Do you love Daddy, Ivy? Do you love Daddy so much?"

I feel my eyes get misty; I kiss the top of Rye's head.

"Yes, you do, don't you?" she continues to coo.

The watch on my wrist vibrates. I check it; text from Clay that reads, *Here!!!!!!!*

"Is that Dad?"" Rye asks.

It always makes me chuckle to remember that Clay Linden is my father-in-law. Dad would be an apt description. "It is. You ready for them?"

She nods excitedly and then looks back at Ivy. "Are you ready to meet your grandma and grandpa, Ivy? Yes, you are."

I start to go toward the door. "I'll be right back."

"Okay," Rye replies, not looking up from Ivy.

I sigh. As if she could get any more beautiful than she

was when I first met her or when she was pregnant and growing, Rye has never looked more beautiful than right now. A mother. It suits her perfectly. "I love you."

"I love you," she says back with a quick smile.

I leave my girls to go fetch our families. Big moment. My heart pounds as I walk the halls of the hospital. I slip my hands into my pockets and begin to spin the wedding ring on my finger. We were married only a few days into the New Year. Still newlyweds. Still new to our relationship even. It doesn't feel like that, though. Feels... solid. Steady.

My heart pounds the closer I get to the lobby. I'm nervous to share this with our families. I've forced them to accept so much in such a short time. And all of them have showed up without fail. The boys have met Rye with love, all of them thrilled that I've found this happiness and that there has been life for me beyond Rose's death. Piper is excited to not be the littlest anymore. And Clay and I have gotten to bond over fatherhood later in life (and grandfatherhood *earlier* than we might have expected). Just as it was back in the day when I was able to help him through the grief of losing Heather. It's things like this that make me realize what kindred spirits we are.

I don't even feel the exhaustion of the past forty-eight hours. Still living on adrenaline and basking in the glow of Ivy's birth, I stride into the lobby where my eyes immediately zero in on Clay and Giselle who are joined by my sons. Keifer's brought along June who is holding Piper as if they're old friends.

"There he is! Proud dad!" Clay announces upon seeing me. He holds a magnificent bouquet of flowers, it's almost embarrassing.

"Hey," I say, suddenly feeling very shy. My best friend is also the father of my wife, grandfather of my newest baby.

"Look at that smile," Giselle says, her smile mirroring mine. Giselle glows. Now five months pregnant, her stomach is becoming more prominent. She embraces me tightly. "Congratulations."

"Thank you," I say.

Clay holds out his hand. We shake and fall into a brotherly embrace. "How is she?" Clay asks.

"Great. She did amazing," I say.

"Yeah?" he confirms, his eyes brightening, already gleaming with tears.

"Yeah, she was... they're both... " I can't say much more, or I'll burst into tears. Looking into his eyes, Rye's eyes, I'm overwhelmed again with gratitude and joy. "Go see her. She's so excited."

Clay and Giselle exchange a smile and then start off to her room, Giselle giving my hand a squeeze as they walk past.

Then, here I am, left with my boys, who are all watching me with tentative smiles. I remember each of their births like it was yesterday. Piper's too. I remember the terror I felt when Jarred was born, feeling so helpless at Rose's side, and Oliver's whose birth was so quick that he was born in the car, and Keifer's which was peaceful and measured, the culmination of what Rose and I had created. While I wasn't in the room when Piper was born, I was in Clay's shoes. Pacing and waiting, until Jarred tore out to see me and collapsed into my arms in tears.

As strange as it is, I wish Rose was here to share this with me. Rye and I wouldn't have found each other without losing her. And yet there's a piece of me that wants to feel her arms around me, wants to hear her whisper, "You did it."

"Hey, Dad," Oliver says.

And that cuts right to my heart. *Dad.* Tears spill down my cheeks. "Hey, guys."

"Grampa! Why are you crying?" Piper yelps.

She reaches to me from June's arms, and I take her, hold her close. "Because I'm so happy, Pipes."

"Aww. You need hugs," Piper replies and presses her face to mine.

"You heard the lady," Jarred says.

One by one, my boys crowd around me. Our group hugs have gotten more frequent in their adulthood as we all try to navigate life beyond their mother. Now, they're here to support me as I become a father once more. I've never been more grateful.

"Come on, let's sit and talk for a bit. Give them some time with Rye before you go meet her," I say as soon as I get my bearings again.

We all go sit together; I hold Piper on my lap closely.

"What's her name?" Jarred asks.

"Ivy Heather-Rose Hawthorn," I say.

"You couldn't settle for one plant, could you? Had to name her after a whole garden," Keifer ribs.

June smacks his knee. "Don't be rude! It's cute!"

"That's really special, Dad," Jarred says with a nod.

"She should be named after me," Piper grumbles.

June laughs, "You're one of a kind, Piper. There can only be one."

Piper giggles and wriggles from my grasp, rushing back over to June. I catch Jarred watching; no doubt a bittersweet feeling seeing his daughter with a woman when she's barely with her mother.

"It'd be weird if your aunt was named after you, Piper," Oliver teases.

"Oliver! Why do you have to make it weird?" Keifer snaps.

"I'm not making it weird! Dad made it weird!" he replies defensively.

I laugh and that gives space for everyone to join in. He's right. I did make it weird. Ivy is Piper's aunt and Giselle and Clay's baby will be Ivy's aunt or uncle. We're all doing it backward.

We talk for another twenty minutes before we make our way up to Rye's room. I peek my head into the room. "How's it going?"

Clay looks up, newborn Ivy in his arms. "Great. So great." He continues to bob up and down, totally infatuated with the little one.

"She's beautiful, Ash," Giselle says. She's flanking Rye in bed, running her hand over her forehead.

"You ready for a few more guests?" I ask Rye.

"Send in the cavalry," she says.

And with that, the boys barrel in with all the enthusiasm they can have while whispering their congratulations. Clay has a hard time giving up the baby, but he gives in once Giselle pokes him in the arm. Ivy does a brilliant job at being passed around like the loveliest little football that's ever been passed.

Finally, that leaves Piper who has been standing with June off the to the side. Outgoing Piper has gone totally silent, hiding her face in June's pant leg.

"She's a little shy, I think," June says, squeezing Piper's hand.

"Hey, Piper. Come sit with me," Rye encourages.

Piper takes a hesitant step forward. I pick her up and gently set her beside Rye. Rye wraps her arm around Piper and the room goes soft. It's been an unspoken joy for us all to watch Rye step into her maternal instincts by connecting with Piper. "Babies make me nervous too," Rye says, holding out her arms for Keifer to return Ivy.

"But you have a baby, Gramma," Piper says, flabbergasted.

I chuckle. Piper started calling Rye "gramma" from the very first family dinner. She just knew instinctually.

"Yes, but she's so tiny and delicate," Rye replies. She resituates Ivy in her arms and Ivy squalls slightly. "And they can be loud too."

Piper gets onto her knees and peers into Rye's arms. Jarred starts to go to aid her, but I hold him back. "It's okay. She's fine."

"She was in your belly?" Piper asks.

"Hard to believe, right?" my wife asks with an ironic smile.

Piper's eyes widen. "Wow."

The room is silent as Piper stares down at Ivy.

"But then I remember that we were all this small. Isn't that crazy? You were this small. And I was this small and your daddy was this small... "

"Daddy! You were this small?" Piper asks as if it's the funniest thing in the world.

Jarred chuckles. "Yes, I was, Pipes."

"And Grampa was this small!" Rye announces.

Piper laughs and claps her hands. The whole room chuckles.

"And we all turned out okay," Rye continues. Her eyes find mine for the briefest moment. Blue full of future. Full of hope. "Better than, I think."

"Definitely," Clay says almost inaudibly. But I hear it.

Rye looks at Piper. "You want to hold her? I'll help."

Piper plays with her fingers for a moment and then nods definitively.

"Okay. Here's how it works."

Rye explains how best to hold a baby. The rest of us do not intercede. It's as if we aren't even there. And ever so slowly, Rye inches baby Ivy into Piper's arms until she's no longer holding her. She props a pillow under Piper's cradling arms.

"You're so good at it, Piper," Rye says softly.

Piper's face splits with the biggest smile she can give. "Look! I'm doing it. Daddy! Grampa! Everyone!"

Everyone looks with awe and wonder. This room full of strange and haphazard connections, all bonding together over my little girl's arrival. I can't imagine anyone's heart is anything but full. And there's so much potential still. Clay and Giselle will welcome their baby in July. Piper will turn four in a month. And my three sons have their futures ahead of them... careers, loves, and so much more.

And Rye and me. We have our baby now.

We have a whole life to start together.

Printed in Great Britain
by Amazon